Also by Kingsley Amis in
Panther Books

I Want It Now
The Green Man
Girl, 20
What Became of Jane Austen? and other questions
On Drink
That Uncertain Feeling
I Like It Here

Kingsley Amis

The Riverside Villas Murder

Panther

Granada Publishing Limited
Special overseas edition published in 1974 by
Panther Books Ltd
Frogmore, St Albans, Herts AL2 2NF

First published in Great Britain in 1973 by
Jonathan Cape Ltd
Copyright © 1973 by Kingsley Amis
Made and printed in Great Britain by
Richard Clay (The Chaucer Press) Ltd
Bungay, Suffolk
Set in Monotype Ehrhardt

CONTENTS

Those who may wish to pit their wits against the author's and solve the mystery for themselves are advised to study pages 61, 82 and 160.

To Jane—again

I

How Mr Hakim Died

'For goodness' sake, Peter, stop ruining your eyes and get out into the fresh air. The first spot of sun we've had for weeks, and you have to sit there poring over that tripe.'

Peter Furneaux looked up from the *Wizard* with hidden reluctance, hidden because not to have hidden it might sharpen his father's mild crossness into anger and accusations of being bolshy, reluctance because 'The Return of the Incas' had reached the point at which the Inca army, having reduced two villages to ash with its gigantic sun-reflecting mirrors, was about to meet its first organized opposition. 'It isn't tripe, Dad, honestly. It's jolly good and jolly exciting.'

'All right, read me a bit. Read me the bit you've just been reading.'

' "Don José Hernandez, whose ancestors had fought the English in the Spanish Armada, was an aristocrat and a gallant soldier, but he was no tactician. Without hesitation he ordered his trumpeter to sound the charge. Sweating and cursing in the blazing heat, the troopers got their sturdy little ponies into a gallop, many ——" '

'That'll do. Got. No educated man ever says got, not in print, anyway. That's the kind of rubbish errand-boys read, always assuming they can read. Board-school boys. Not a lad at Blackfriars Grammar.'

'Mr Taylor says you can say got. Write it as well, I mean. He says there's no rule says you can't.' Peter spoke very mildly.

His father sighed and, with his left hand, knocked out his pipe into a copper ashtray incorporated into a strip of suede that was draped over the arm of the chair. 'Does he, now? Does he, indeed? And how old is your Mr Taylor?'

'I don't know. About twenty-five or thirty.'

'A young man, in fact.'

'Yes, I suppose so.'

'And no doubt he considers he knows everything.'

'Well, he doesn't go on as if he does.'

'In that case, given his age, he's by way of being a rarity,' said Captain Furneaux with conviction. 'A jewel of goodly price. Mr Taylor won't get very far in the world of today. Where it's bounce that counts.'

Peter resigned himself to some development of this favourite theme of his father's, but without much inner groaning. Better by far an account of what old Trench at the Ratepayers' Association, old Partridge at the central office, his father himself felt about the world of today than have the *Wizard* consigned (for a week or two anyhow) to the catalogue of forbidden reading-matter, there to join the works of Aldous Huxley, W. Somerset Maugham and other unhealthy influences. But, as happened about one time out of four, his father abruptly dropped his discontented tone, grinned widely enough to show his gold-filled upper molar, and said with a good-humoured air,

'Still, no point in my talking your hind leg off when I've just gone for you for keeping indoors. What about giving yourself a few minutes' catching practice on the Meadow while I rustle up a spot of grub? Then it'll be time to ring your mother up and find out how she's getting on over there.'

'I thought I might take the plane out.'

'The aeroplane,' said Captain Furneaux, still good-humouredly.

'Sorry, yes, the aeroplane.'

'Get along with you then, old boy. I'll give you a cooee when it's ready.'

At the top of the single flight of stairs, Peter paused, as he usually did, to look through the circular landing-window across the back garden to the river—well, you were supposed to call it the river, though it was more like a large brook; too small for any real boats, and too fast and turbulent for his Toc-Toc motor-cruiser. But having it there, being able to walk along its bank, was marvellous, especially in the hour before dusk.

From the deal table beside his bed he collected his Morane-Saulnier N mid-wing monoplane, or rather the rough $\frac{1}{24}$-scale flying model of that aircraft which he had put together, laboriously and with some paternal help, from a five-shilling construction kit. Then, after another pause, he picked up his green Skyhawk glider and its capapult. In the interval, he had considered and rejected the notion that the game he proposed playing with these two devices might be thought childish or destructive or both. What did he care? And besides, anybody who just happened to see him playing would almost certainly not understand the game anyway.

He went out by the front door of Montrose, alternatively 19 Riverside Villas, and caught sight of Mr Langdon doing something to a rose-bush in the fives-court-sized front garden of Ottery St Mary, or No. 11. At the sound of the door closing he looked up and waved cheerfully to Peter, who thought him a nice and very funny man. The imitations he did were terrific, especially the ones of Sydney Howard and C. H. Middleton. Peter's father often said that if you closed your eyes you would absolutely think it was the real chap, and that Mr Langdon ought to be on the wireless.

Returning the wave, Peter moved on to the coarse grass of the Meadow. As in the case of the river, this was not really a meadow, though it might at some stage have been part of one: it was an irregular green about as long as a football field and not quite as wide, separating the two lines of semi-detached villas. A man from the Council came and mowed it from time to time, but on this Sunday evening at the end of May it was thick with flowering clumps of butter-cups, dandelions and other presumable weeds whose names Peter did not know.

He was fourteen years old, not tall for his age, with fair hair brushed diagonally off his brow, a fair skin unmarked by adolescent eruptions, and sound teeth which Captain Furneaux's frequently expressed attitude to sweet-eating had done something to put in that state. Peter's looks in general were of the sort that had two or three times led strange men, encountered on the train to and from school or while waiting for it, to take an undue interest in him. That interest had always proved momentary as well as undue, for Peter had no inhibitions about using his wide vocabulary of swear-words and other offensive expressions, at full volume where necessary. Nor did such incidents trouble him in the least, which they might have done had he not known with some exactitude what such men had in mind.

He had found out at first hand in hurried dealings with two of his form-mates and more leisurely ones with a third boy who lived in another part of the town. Strange men were perverts and disgusting; what Peter did with his friends was regarded by them all, in a ready consensus, as quite okay (as well as very enjoyable) because they only did

it because they could not get girls yet and until they could
get girls. Getting girls was a long-term objective, which
meant it had to be worked at all the time. How you worked
at it had been elaborately devised by one Forester, a fifth-
former at the Grammar who had once, without any sense of
incongruity being felt by either, tried unsuccessfully to kiss
Peter in the school cloakroom.

Forester called his recommendations the Code of Dishonour. The degree of actual success it brought him was
never very clear, but he gave it some air of authenticity by
his small collection of genuine French dirty postcards and
his habit of carrying several contraceptives in his hip-
pocket as a matter of routine. Boys still talked of the time
he had shown a packet of them to one of the girls who
worked in the tuck-shop and made her cry. Whatever
Forester's further performance might be, there was no
doubt at all of the popularity of his Code. No quasi-docu-
ment since the American Declaration of Independence
could have won such immediate and profound assent. *Find
one*, the Code began—it did tend to take almost nothing for
granted, which was probably a factor in the breadth of its
appeal. Then, *Keep on at her until she lets you take her
out, but don't touch her until you've got her really on her
own.* This, or rather the first half of this, was the section
which Peter was now on his way to try to do something
about.

He had found one several months before, one called
Daphne Hodgson who, a few weeks earlier still, had come
with her parents and older brother and younger sister to live
at 22 Riverside Villas, then recently completed. (It was a bit
thick to call that row of houses, on the far side of the
Meadow, Riverside anything, but people who owned things
and so on always seemed to count successfully on nobody

objecting, like boarding-houses called Seaview only someone with X-ray eyes could see the tiniest bit of sea from.)
Anyway, Daphne was fifteen. The magnitude of the age-
gap between her and Peter made for difficulty, both
because he would be competing, if he ever got to the stage
of competing, with fellows of sixteen and seventeen, and
because she was just older. But the difficulty had its advantages: it would make success twice as creditable, and even
Forester, unless in an unusually fanatical mood, would
grant that it would make failure less blameworthy. The
same reasoning applied to the fact that Daphne was pretty
to a slightly scaring extent.

Peter thought about all this while, the Skyhawk tucked
tail-first into his blazer pocket and his index finger busy
twirling the Morane-Saulnier's prop to wind up its elastic,
he walked through the rank herbage to a spot from which
he could see if Daphne was about and yet not appear to
have this in mind. The signs were quite good: a striped
deck-chair stood on the tiny front lawn of No. 22 behind
the privet hedge and what must be a library book lay open
and face down on the canvas seat. Either Daphne or her
mother, most likely, was in mid-read. With a parade of concentration, Peter finished his winding—he would have to
invest soon in one of those new geared rotators which a full
week's strict embezzlement of his dinner-money would put
within his reach—and prepared for a launch. Just a recce
the first time, a circle round the area to observe enemy troop
concentrations and movements of ammunition and other
supplies.

He adjusted rudder and ailerons, then, there being no
chance of a ground take-off on this terrain, pushed the
Morane-Saulnier gently into the air at shoulder height.
What followed went a long way beyond his expectations. As

intended, the machine performed a climbing turn, levelled
out into a wide curve and, losing height now, returned to
within a few yards of its launching-point, but, seconds later,
it skimmed No. 22's hedge and came to a sudden stop in a
clump of wallflowers under the window at near enough the
very moment when Daphne Hodgson, a glass of what
looked like fizzy lemonade in her hand, appeared at the open
front door.

This was indeed too much too soon. What Peter had
been hoping for was opportunity for a gradual approach, a
zig-zag homing-in followed in due time by an exchange of
hallos. (He had been hoping more ardently, though less
consciously, that Daphne would not emerge at all and that
he would thus have gone some way towards discharging
that day's obligations under the Code without having
actually had to do anything.) But there was no turning back
now. He walked at a moderate pace over to the garden gate,
which, in colour and design, looked like something on the
Southern Railway.

Sucking at her lemonade through a pair of straws,
Daphne stared at him as he came up. Her large bright blue
eyes always stared, never looked. She was wearing a boy's
blue-and-white striped shirt, perhaps borrowed from her
brother Geoff, and the light-blue Daks trousers Peter had
seen her in more than once before. Among the several
exceptions Captain Furneaux took to the Hodgson family
—the chief and fundamental one being that Mr Hodgson
had played no active part in the War 'for reasons best known
to himself'—these trousers came oddly high on the list:
they were quite unsuitable for a child (child?) of that age,
and were to do with flaunting something unspecified. Peter
himself found this illogical: trousers hid the whole of a
girl's legs while a skirt showed quite a bit, now and then

quite a lot, of them. At the same time, it had to be admitted that Daphne's trousers added a third place, somewhere about the bottom of her stomach or the tops of the insides of her legs, to the permanent two which it embarrassed him to be caught looking towards, her eyes and her, well, breasts, as they were called in books. Peter reached the gate and, trying to unfocus his own eyes, said clearly,

'Hallo, Daphne. Can I fetch my aeroplane?'

'Your what?'

'Aeroplane. There in the ——'

'Oh,' said Daphne. It was her favourite word, probably because she could make it mean so many different things and keep them all so separate from each other. This time it meant that she was very slightly surprised to find anyone at all, even a kid, using the same word for a toy and the piece of complicated grown-up machinery that every half-hour or so carried actual people to and from, for instance, Croydon Aerodrome a few miles away. She said it, as always, without seeming to mind or even notice the lower-class accent she said everything she said in, illustrating another exception Peter's father took to her and her family, one which Peter saw and understood without caring. She said nothing else.

'Can I fetch it?'

'Why not?'

He lifted the latch and went up the few yards of gravel path, feeling as if he had a whole theatre audience staring at him instead of just one girl. It took a few moments to free the Morane-Saulnier, with its easily torn fuselage and wing sections, from among the stems.

'Smashed up, is it?'

'No, it's okay. It'd have to go full speed into a brick wall to do much to itself. It's very light, you see.'

'Oh.' This time she made it sound as if she were about to fall asleep, or even actually had.

'Here, feel it.'

'I believe you.'

'What are you reading?' asked Peter after hardly any pause at all.

'Book.'

'Oh.' This slipped out; he felt (because he was still not really looking at her) a change in the quality of her stare. She moved off the step and past him, well within his arm's length if he had cared to reach out and grab her. But he did not. It was funny how Daphne in the flesh was even prettier than Daphne thought about, and yet less something or other at the same time, less whatever it was that made it so easy, so inescapable, almost, to imagine himself doing far more than grab her, a habit of his when he woke up in the mornings, for instance, and quite often for the two or three minutes after that. Had she done it? Some of them had, some of them did, and Daphne must have been asked to more often than most of them. But now, as she picked up her book and settled herself in the deck-chair, it was impossible to imagine her doing it with anybody.

Peter just got in before she started reading. 'Is it a thriller?'

'Not so far it isn't.'

'What's it called?'

With a fair grace, Daphne glanced at the running title. '*The Constant* ... ' She hesitated.

'*Nymph*,' said Peter, looking over her shoulder from what he considered a daringly close position, and then trying to see down the front of her shirt. Some time later he added, 'What's it about?' in a voice that sounded to him like a gramophone record starting to run down.

'Girl in love with an old man. I think.'

'Would you like to come out for a walk after supper?'

'Where to?'

'Oh, just along the river.'

'What for? You get gnats there.'

'Not much.'

'Enough, though. Anyway, what for? I don't like walks when I'm not going anywhere. No point in it.'

'We could talk and things.'

'Some things. When's your voice going to break?'

'It's started to already, and a lot else is all there in working order,' said Peter, stoutly implementing *Bring up sex whenever you can, but not in a crude way*.

'I don't know what you're talking about.' Daphne spoke with animation for the first time.

'I bet. What about this walk?'

'What walk? I told you.'

'All right. I'll try again, though. I don't give up easily.'

'Oh.'

As Peter shut the gate behind him and strolled back on to the Meadow, he was visited by an emotion he rarely felt—envy: envy of Daphne's self-containment and also of her having a brother and a sister, of their all having a detective for a father (instead of an estate agent's local representative, as in Peter's own case), of what he imagined the life of the whole family to be like. Being an only child did not mean that you were by yourself too much; on the contrary, you got the whole of your parents reserved for just you instead of divided up into three, say. Peter liked his father, but would have preferred on the whole to have him as an uncle, even one living in the same house. His mother he quite loved, but there again she talked to him about a lot of things he could not remember afterwards, even the next minute. He would not have minded changing places for a time with his cousin George; forfeiting three precious years of progress towards being grown-up might not be such a bad swap for acquiring a younger brother, however much of a pest a child of that age (eight) might be to have round the house—plus whichever it was Auntie Peggy was on the point of producing over at Mitcham. Peter rather wished he had been allowed to go with his mother when she went there three days previously, but it had been decided without any trouble that he should stay and keep his father company instead.

The sun, low down over the river, brightened a little, and Peter found he had almost finished rewinding the motor of the Morane-Saulnier. Dishonour was satisfied: he could forget all about Daphne and get on with the game he had had in mind from the start. He sent the monoplane off as before on a climbing turn, then quickly pulled the Skyhawk and its catapult from his pocket and launched the glider on an interception course. As usual, he found he had aimed off too far: the one passed a good ten feet in front of the nose of the other, but he had judged the height well and the pilot of the Morane-Saulnier, had there been one outside Peter's imagination, would undoubtedly have had a nasty shock at the sight of an aerial torpedo flashing across his bows.

The powered aircraft made a rough-and-ready but undamaged landing in a patch of long grass; the unpowered one was further away and, although he had kept his eye on it as it fell, not to be found at once, being smaller and also green in colour. There it was; he picked it up; just then he heard his name called and Mrs Trevelyan of No. 21, the house next to his and the last in the row, was coming down her garden path in his direction.

Even Forester would hardly have thought of remarking that Peter was having a good deal of luck round about now

in the way attractive girls kept coming on the scene as soon
as he went anywhere. Mrs Trevelyan was certainly attractive, but she was definitely not a girl. What she was it was
less easy to be categorical about. She was not a woman,
being not only too young but also not like the newsagent's
wife or the person wearing a pink-and-white apron who did
the nastier parts of serving out the teas at the tennis club on
Saturdays (and all the clearing up afterwards). Nor was Mrs
Trevelyan a young woman, one of a group that belonged to
his grandfather's time or to books or both. Neighbour's
wife, nice, well-spoken little thing in her late twenties or
thereabouts, would have been Captain Furneaux's description. Peter saw the justice of it while both more vividly and
more vaguely seeing a good deal of what it left out, such as
the intensely black centre-parted hair, the very dark brown
eyes, the way her shoulders and the rest of her top half and
her hips moved about without her seeming to know under
her white dress with the patterns of red and blue flowers on
it, and things like that.

She greeted him with the easy cordiality he whole-
heartedly responded to and liked her for, feelings very distant from the uneasy, intermittent, not fully acknowledged
desire to be close to her, in fact as close as possible, a desire
sharper at its sharpest than anything he had experienced in
Daphne's presence. 'Hallo, Peter, how are you? Any news
from your mother?' Her voice was rather high in pitch and
rather quiet, making her seem younger.

'Very well, thank you, Mrs Trevelyan. No, nothing
since yesterday. We're going to ring up soon and find
out.'

'I was wondering, when you've done that, whether you
and your father might like to come and have a bite of
supper with my husband and me.'

'It's very kind of you, Mrs Trevelyan, but I think Dad's started to cook something already.'

'I'll give him a knock and try and stop him.' But she made no move towards Montrose; instead, she came right up to Peter, glanced unemphatically at the Morane-Saulnier and the Skyhawk, and asked, with just the right mixture of lightness and well-acted professional interest, 'Manœuvres?'

'Just training flights. Routine.' He did not want to seem childishly eager.

'Of course, I realize you can't give anything away to casual inquirers. I just wondered ... '

'Well ... actually these are secret trials. A new technique of anti-aircraft defence.'

'Really?'

'An aerial torpedo'—he held up the Skyhawk—'aimed at the middle of an enemy formation. The real thing would have a time fuse as well as a contact fuse, like an ordinary anti-aircraft shell, but it would do much more damage than that because it could carry a lot of T.N.T.'

'Yes. How's it fired?'

'It'd be launched by catapult. This one's just a model, but already there are catapults, real ones I mean, that can launch aeroplanes from the decks of naval vessels. The battle-cruiser H.M.S. *Hood* has got one. They could easily be adapted.'

Mrs Trevelyan moved a step closer, and with the movement he sensed that the direction of her interest had changed. 'Do you build your own machines, Peter?'

'The gliders, they're two a penny, I mean this type's fourpence, but there are bigger and smaller ones,' he said rapidly, looking past her, not because she might be staring at him, like Daphne, but because he felt or half-saw her looking at him; well, more looking him over. He went on no less rapidly, 'The plane, the aeroplane's just a shop kit, elastic motor, quite powerful when it's fully wound, but there are petrol ones you can buy, but they cost a terrific lot.' Was Mr Langdon watching? No, he had evidently finished with his rose-bush and gone indoors. 'I would like to build one of my own, but that would cost a lot too, and I'm not sure I could do it anyhow. Not good enough with my hands.'

Peter felt himself blushing as much as if Mrs Trevelyan had been thinking he was silly, which he was quite sure she had not been. She had just gone on looking at him in a way that reminded him now of a man who had, correctly and so taking threepence of his pocket-money off him, guessed his weight at a fair the previous summer, and yet not quite like that.

'I'm sure that sort of thing develops with practice.' (She was smiling, he saw, but still not thinking he was silly.) 'Now I must go and find your father before he puts the potatoes on. Are you coming in?'

'I think I'll just have another couple of flights.'

'Oh, I'll hope to see you later, then.'

Ten minutes afterwards, Peter re-entered the sitting-room. Captain Furneaux, who had the *Sunday Express* open on his lap, looked up over his horn-rimmed spectacles and scowled at him, but he knew his father well enough to be able to see at once that the source of the scowl was something the world, not Peter, had done or left undone. A profession of ignorance of what that world was coming to would very likely be on the way.

'Honestly, old boy, I can't imagine what possesses some people, really I can't. I've tried, but I can't.'

'What sort of people, Dad?'

'Well, this ... woman, what's her name? ... Charlotte

Bryant, sentenced to death yesterday at Dorchester for murdering her husband with arsenic. Weed-killer, if you please. Of course, the creature was illiterate, had to be told what an inquest was, all sorts of gipsy fellows hanging round her. Scum of the earth, you can imagine. But still, giving your own husband arsenic, over a period of about six months, too. Watching him writhing about—very painful, apparently. I just can't understand it. Beyond me.'

After a sufficient pause, Peter asked, 'Are we going to have supper with Mr and Mrs Trevelyan?'

'Yes, you'd better nip up in a minute and have a sluice and put on a clean shirt and a pair of longs. Decent little woman, Mrs Trevelyan. I can't say I altogether take to Don or Ron or whatever he's called. Bit of a go-getter, if you ask me.'

Captain Furneaux spoke without the emphasis he normally used for such pronouncements. Folding the paper and putting it under his right arm, he got unhurriedly to his feet from the brass-studded leather armchair. He was a man in his early forties (or so Peter had estimated, never having been told), beaky-nosed, with greying brown hair brushed straight back, a squareish figure in navy-blue cardigan and dark-grey flannel trousers. He would have given an impression of some physical power had it not been for that right arm, which, as the result of a wartime injury, hung loosely from the shoulder—not uselessly, for he retained some control of the upper muscles and could flex the wrist, use the hand for light tasks, even write for a few minutes at a time. But his tennis-playing days were far behind him, a sad deprivation for one who had been a minor champion in his youth. Peter would try to feel the force of this when his father went on about the tennis club, of which he was honorary secretary, told the story, not always to people who had never heard it before, of the flying accident in Mesopotamia that had done the damage, or simply had an attack of what he called the blues. At the moment, standing on the supposedly bearskin rug with his back to the unlit gas-fire, he seemed in danger of such an attack, though perhaps was no more than preoccupied. He frowned, then raised his eyebrows and pouted. Presently he said,

'This chap they hanged just the other week, Buck Ruxton. Not his real name, of course: he was called Mr Hakim originally. Parsee gentleman. Still, even so, he was a doctor, they let him practise in this country, must have been a fellow of some education, more than I ever had in all probability, not like that Bryant creature. And what does he do? Goes for his lady friend and the nursemaid with an axe or something and then ... well, no need to go into that. Did you read about it?'

'No,' lied Peter.

'You wouldn't want to, old boy, believe me. But I ask you! Just going for his lady friend because they didn't get on. It beats me hollow, I tell you frankly. People who do things like that must be barmy. I can't see anything else for it.'

'Dad?'

'Mm?'

'Are we going to ring up Mum?'

'Yes. Oh yes, you go and ask for the number, if you would, and I'll come and speak when they've put you through.'

Peter rather disliked the telephone, to him a comparative novelty, but he went out into the hall readily enough, stooped over the instrument, which stood on a low polished table between some tulips in a vase and a lavishly mounted and framed photograph of Captain

Furneaux in Royal Flying Corps uniform, and took the
receiver off its hook. While he waited for the operator
to answer him, he heard his father give a kind of groaning sigh from the sitting-room, in fact, as one who lived
in the house could tell immediately, from the spot by
the fireplace where he had taken his stance two minutes
or more earlier. It was not a habit of his to stay so long
apparently lost in thought, Peter just had time to reflect
before the expected click and voice in his ear drove the tiny
incident from his mind, though not from his memory.

II

The Disappearance of Boris Karloff

The local museum occupied a room at the rear of the public library: its contents were not extensive enough to warrant their being housed in a separate building. They consisted largely of old, or at least far from new, books and pamphlets (no doubt the reason for the original choice of site) that hardly anyone ever bothered to look at. There were likenesses of three or four of the town's few and not very noteworthy worthies, some coins of no great age or rarity, and other odds and ends, all similarly disregarded. But there was also Longbarrow Man, whom, though he was not as famous as Piltdown Man, a lot of people bothered to come and look at, most of them from London, true, a bare dozen miles to the north-west, but some from further afield, and one, once, all the way from a place called Princeton in America, though, true again, he had not left his native land solely for that purpose.

Longbarrow Man had been disinterred, only four years previously, in the course of blasting for a new chalk quarry at the edge of the town. His return to the land of the living had, at a time when hard news was scanty and what there was of it grim, caused a fair-sized sensation and much excited theorizing. He was in rapid succession probably Stone Age, possibly Viking, beyond all question Roman, conceivably Bronze Age, most likely a Victorian murder victim, perhaps an Ancient Briton, demonstrably a fake, demonstrably genuine, whatever he might genuinely be. Somebody who was something to do with the British

26

Museum, and therefore an expert, had laid controversy to rest by writing an article (off-prints on sale at the library counter, price 6*d*.) that disproved all extant theories about Longbarrow Man's provenance while, after the fashion of experts, offering nothing at all by way of a tenable theory. In similar vein, the supposed long barrow involved was left with no more than a shred or two of its claim to have been a primeval grave-mound, and at the same time the notion that such a topographical feature could have come about by accident was vigorously assailed.

What was undisputed about Longbarrow Man started with the fact that he was a skeleton, one so excellently preserved that the first response of all to his reappearance had been a police inquiry, hastily instituted and soon discontinued. In his original resting-place he had worn, and under his glass case in the library back room still wore, a rough necklet of stones technically describable as semi-precious; the even rougher rings that had become separated from his fingers had been restored to his finger-bones; he wore metal bracelets of sorts too. Whatever interest might attach to him and his accoutrements, neither he nor they had proved to be worth much in hard cash, not quite enough, anyway, for the Town Council to have decided to part with this modest local attraction. Nevertheless, some time on the Wednesday–Thursday night following Peter Furneaux's aerial-torpedo trials, an unknown person took the trouble to steal Longbarrow Man (and his accoutrements) from under the glass case. Whoever it was also stole some, though not all, of the coins on display in the museum.

The theft was discovered shortly after nine o'clock on the Thursday morning by the Assistant Librarian, a Miss Houlgate, who immediately informed the police, and, as soon as possible thereafter, Mr McGrath, the Librarian

himself. By half-past nine, she and he and two officials of
the County Constabulary, Sergeant Duke and P.C.
Hawkins, were assembled at the scene of the burglary.
After a brief examination, and the taking of a formal statement from Miss Houlgate, Duke left Hawkins on guard and
returned to the police station. Partly as a result of his report,
Detective-Constable Barrett of the County C.I.D. paid a
call on the Acting Chief Constable, Colonel R. P. W.
Manton, D.S.O., M.C., towards eleven-thirty that same
morning.

Barrett was twenty-eight, with seven years' service in the
Force behind him but only a few months' in criminal investigation. He had been one of the first graduates of the Hendon
Police College, founded a couple of years earlier by Lord
Trenchard, Chief Commissioner of the Metropolitan
Police. A serious-minded, ambitious young man, Barrett
was eager to prove himself, to bring off some feat of detec-
tion that would win him professional advancement and
silence, among his immediate colleagues at least, the fairly
friendly ridicule attaching to the Hendon boy wonders. The
purloining of Boris Karloff, as Longbarrow Man was
known throughout the area, and of a handful of old coins
seemed unlikely, on the face of it, to bring him the hoped-
for chance of displaying his deductive powers to real
advantage.

Only on the face of it, however. Barrett had been
thoroughly schooled in the importance of keeping an open
mind until the full facts of a case were ascertained. Such
facts of this case as he had learnt at the police station certainly pointed in the rough direction of a practical joke of
some sort, part of a student rag (though there were no
students in that sense nearer than London), perhaps the
fulfilment of a bet—in short, an unserious crime. As against

this, there was the matter of the coins. Stealing Boris
Karloff might very well be the work of a joker or a crank; it
was hard to see the stealing of the coins as anything but
straight theft for gain.

Barrett considered these points in the passenger's seat of
the police Austin Six while it carried him the easy distance
to Colonel Manton's house just outside the town—only a
few hundred yards, as it happened, from where Longbarrow
Man had been unearthed. Some consideration of points was
advisable before encountering Colonel Manton, with whom,
or rather at a safe distance from whom, Barrett had worked
on an arson case the previous autumn, just after joining the
C.I.D. The Acting Chief Constable acted for the Chief
Constable, an ailing retired general now on one of his
extended trips to the Continent, far too often for the liking
of anyone on the county Force, and too vigorously as well.
This habit of vigour, or of ruddy nosey-parker slave-driv-
ing, as it was called by Detective-Inspector Cox, Barrett's
superior, was the other half of the reason why this call was
being paid so promptly, or perhaps at all, and the whole of
the reason why Cox had ordered Barrett to pay it instead of
paying it himself or sending a detective-sergeant. He had
told Barrett, by way of farewell, that he was sick and tired
of the old busybody's most often invoked standing order,
the one which said he (the old busybody) must be informed
without delay of any infraction of the law in his jurisdiction
more serious than drunk and disorderly, and had added that
he (Cox) would take time off during a lovely day of paper-
work to wonder how he (Barrett) was standing up to the job
of staying sane.

The house stood apart from others at the end of its
road, near the point where that road became an unmade
track winding over a low range of grassy, treeless hills. It

was a substantial red-brick building, double-fronted in
Barrett's terminology, and, in his estimation, not very old,
though older than its neighbours, which must have been
put up since the War. Colonel Manton lived in it alone;
he had a housekeeper who came in by the day; he had no
wife, nor had ever had one; according to Cox, he was the
sort of man who would not have known what to do with a
wife. Barrett, who did not really care for Cox, paid no
attention to such talk. He was aware of something of what
Colonel Manton had done in the last spring of the War at
the battle of the Lys, of how, though severely wounded, he
had rallied his shattered battalion and led it in a counter-
attack until fainting from loss of blood—was aware of
enough, at any rate, to regard him with respect.

A medium-sized, slight figure in a brown suit, his nearly
bald crown concealed under a green pork-pie hat, Barrett
got out of the car, asked the driver to wait out of sight but
within hearing, and went up to the front door of the house.
Swinging the bright brass knocker, he felt a small twinge of
excitement. The Boris Karloff business might lead to nothing at all, but it was markedly different from talking to
informers short of information or shopkeepers who might
have, but very seldom had, seen items of stolen property.

The left-hand half of the double door opened and there
appeared the fat little housekeeper he remembered from a
previous visit. She took his hat, showed him into the
library he likewise remembered, said she would tell the
colonel of his arrival and went away. The library was a high-
ceilinged room with much oak panelling, a baby grand
piano, a large radio-gramophone, few and indistinguishable
pictures, and a great many books, tightly packed on open
shelves and overflowing on to tables and chairs. Barrett was
a keen reader, mainly of serious stuff like biographies, his-

tory and war memoirs. He seized the chance he had not had before, of finding out something about the Acting Chief Constable by finding out what he read.

At first glance, the collection was unprepossessing, the greater part still in their jackets (many of a garish yellow), the visible bindings cheap and often scuffed. The first authors' names Barrett happened to come across were unfamiliar: John Dickson Carr, John Rhode, Anthony Berkeley. Nor were the first titles any help: *The House of the Arrow*, *The Nine Tailors*, *The Incredulity of Father Brown*—fancy some-one writing a whole book about a parson's incredulity. Then Barrett caught sight of *The Mysterious Affair at Styles*, by Agatha Christie, and knew where he was: he ought to have guessed the old boy would be a 'tec-yarn fan. Interesting, but a little disappointing—what fiction he had time for himself came from real authors like Hugh Walpole or J. B. Priestley. Across the room were a couple of rows of better-bound volumes, but he only had time to glimpse one title —*Medical Jurisprudence*—before Colonel Manton came briskly into the room.

The colonel was fifty, but he looked several years younger. His black hair, cut short and unmarked with grey, was more abundant than Barrett's, and if anything he was slimmer than Barrett, too. The skin of his face was close to the bones, giving a slightly skull-like effect; his expression, perpetually on the verge, it seemed, of breaking into a wide smile, blended the genial and the sardonic. He was wearing (among other things) a tweed suit with matching waistcoat, a beautifully knotted woollen tie, and gleaming tan-coloured shoes.

'Good morning to you, Barrett. Wretched weather.' Colonel Manton's voice, coming from far back in the mouth, was deep and rasping, but clear, the sort of voice that

(Barrett imagined) would when raised carry well across a parade-ground. As it was, something in the tone invited him to consider the weather more closely than ever before in his life.

'Good morning, sir. Yes, it has been showery. Unsettled, like.'

'Indeed. Do sit down.' The colonel looked at the watch on his bony wrist. 'What would you say to a glass of champagne?'

This question nearly froze Barrett stiff in the act of sitting down on an upright chair which he had picked out as suitable to his status. He would have been quite as well prepared for being asked what he would say to a gold brick or a trip in a submarine. All he said was, 'Well, I ... '

Now the colonel did smile, showing a lot of square teeth. 'Now then, Barrett,' he said in a tone of teasing good-humour, 'don't let's have any of your regimental nonsense about not drinking on duty. If I don't mind, which I clearly don't, the only person who could object is the Home Secretary, and he isn't here. Is he? Don't you agree that a glass of bubbly is a splendid pick-me-up at this time of day?'

Barrett had never tasted champagne, which to him was something that happened in films and at other people's weddings; there had been beer and cider at his own. 'To tell you the truth, sir, I haven't had much practice with it.'

'That we must remedy.' The colonel went to a large bell-button next to the fireplace and pressed it in a complicated way, long-short, long-short. 'Charlie,' he said off-handedly.

'Charlie, sir?'

'I do beg your pardon, I'm getting so bad at judging people's ages. Of course you're far too young. Charlie is Service language for the letter C, which is dash-dot dash-dot in the Morse code, and in this case stands for champagne. Mrs Ellington, who let you in, and I have worked out quite a useful system. Sometimes one does run into complications. For instance, when I want my tea brought I can't just send Toc, the letter T that's to say, because it's nothing more than a single dash, like an ordinary ring meaning she's to come in. So I have to send the whole word, do you see, but it's only dash, dot, dot-dash. Yes, it's a useful system. It saves time for both of us, and it means I only have to see her once on each occasion instead of twice, which is an advantage because I don't like her much. Now for goodness' sake get yourself off that awful chair'—the note of rasping raillery was back—'and find something more comfortable. This isn't an inquisition.'

Barrett sat down at one end of a chesterfield covered in green and black stripes. The colonel remained on his feet in a close approach to the stand-at-ease position.

'Right,' he went on. 'Tell me what you know about this business. All I know is that somebody's snaffled Boris Karloff and some coins.'

Just when Barrett had finished obeying this order, Mrs Ellington came in carrying an opened half-bottle of champagne and two expensive-looking glasses on a silver tray. Without a word, movement or glance from her master, she put them down on a small round table and withdrew. Colonel Manton poured and brought a glass over to Barrett, who started to get up.

'No no no, stay where you are, man. We can't have you popping up and down like a jack-in-the-box.'

'Thank you, sir. Good health.'

'Bung-ho, Barrett.' It sounded indulgent, also ridiculous.

Barrett sipped cautiously. The drink seemed to him prickly and sharp. He wondered for a moment if he should utter a word or two of lying appreciation, until instinct told him that not only would the colonel not be deceived, but might think any comment improper. He drank again.

'How long has Mrs Ellington been with you, sir?'

'Thirteen years, and you mean why do I keep her if I don't like her much. Because I've no reason to believe I'd like anybody else any better. That's why. In all, I suppose I must have interviewed a dozen women before I made my choice, and I only picked this one because of her name.'

After another pause, during which Barrett's mind raced briefly in different directions, he said, 'And it's not everywhere you'd find someone like that you could learn the Morse code.'

'Indeed.' The colonel gave his ambiguous smile. He took a cigarette out of a silver case, put it into a bamboo holder and lit it with a silver lighter. 'How's my old associate Detective-Inspector Cox?'

'All right, I think, sir,' said Barrett, waving out the match he had applied to his own Craven A. 'Busy, as usual.'

'Yes, I can see he sent you instead of coming himself. What did he say to you about that?'

'Well: I'm to get as far as I can on my own, with you that is, sir, and he'll take a hand if—if I get stuck, sir.'

'I see. Economy of effort. His effort.'

'He said it'll either be dead easy, the case, or hopeless.'

'Not a bad snap judgment. Intelligent fellow, Cox. It's a pity he's such a fearful swine.'

Barrett very soon gave up the job of thinking of something to say to that.

The colonel made a sideways movement with his cigarette and holder. 'Now come on, Barrett, stop lingering over your tipple like an old clubman. We've work to do.'

Obediently, Barrett gulped champagne and held out his

glass to be topped up. So it was not true that the more expensive the drink, the longer you were supposed to take over it. 'You want to go down the library and look round, sir?'

'Where else? Knock that back.'

A minute later, after another transmission by way of the bell-button, the colonel had been helped on with a fawn-coloured Burberry and Barrett given his hat. The front door shut behind the two men. Dull sunshine lay across the abundant shrubs and trees to left and right and beyond the short semi-circular drive. A bird twittered. Barrett belched quietly to himself.

'We'll go down in my car,' said Colonel Manton. He made it sound as if in doing so they might well come under fire from machine-guns and minniewerfers, but were not the sort to heed such trifles. 'It has all my magnifying-glasses and false beards and reference books about bicycle tyres and tattoo marks in it,' he added with an emphatic rasp, making that bit sound as if he had it in for somebody or something by no means easy to identify, or perhaps was simply off his head. Barrett mentioned his own means of transport and was told to send it away.

By the time he had obeyed and returned, the colonel had backed a glistening light-grey Jaguar saloon out of a garage built on to the side of his house. He now wore a pair of gauntlets terminating not far short of the elbows, but had evidently abjured the use of goggles, at any rate for local journeys. He drove them fast, skilfully and in silence down past a great many houses that changed from rich-looking to not-rich-looking and back to rich-looking as they moved towards the main London–Eastbourne road, which unfortunately included the whole of the town's High Street. They turned into it. The Methodist chapel, the dame-school, the

Savoy cinema came up, then Woolworth's and the new garage, finally the public library. Colonel Manton parked the Jaguar at the kerb.

Barrett soon got through his investigations, which did no more than fill out Sergeant Duke's preliminary report, and made his way over much green linoleum to the Librarian's office on the first floor. Here the colonel, standing, with his hands clasped in front of him this time, and Mr McGrath, seated at his stained, peeling desk, were conferring over some document.

'Well, Barrett,' said the colonel, 'we're both agog to hear what you've found. Have you made any sensational discoveries?'

'No, sir. As we already knew, the thief got in through the side window in the alley. He ——'

'That means a door-to-door inquiry in the neighbourhood. He could theoretically have been seen.'

'No, sir, the window's in a sort of recess. He couldn't have been seen by anyone who might have been passing the entrance to the alley.'

'While he was actually getting in or out, perhaps not. But he could theoretically have been seen arriving or leaving. Door-to-door inquiry, Barrett. Grit your teeth. You won't find anything, of course.'

'But there must be ——'

'Anything to add to what Duke said about the window itself?'

'Not really, no. Wrapping-paper glued to the pane just above the catch, then a hammer or something. The paper prevents ——'

'May I say something?' This was Mr McGrath, a middle-aged man whose accent, style of dress and thick purple hands made it difficult, for Barrett, to imagine him having any other use for a book than as the traditional table-leg adjunct.

'Certainly, McGrath,' said the colonel, for some reason, one that escaped Barrett, leaving out the final 'th' sound of the name.

'Well, if you go smashing a window with a hammer in the middle of the night, then somebody's going to hear you, even if the pieces don't fall—I follow that. I mean, there was a person sleeping not twenty foot away, in the house on the far side.'

'Barrett will be talking to the person. Won't you, Barrett? But I think the hammer will have been padded. Or a gloved fist would do it.'

'I agree, sir. A pro job, it looks like.'

'It looks like it, yes. Now fingerprints.'

'None on the glass case, sir. You can tell that in two minutes.'

'That case is wiped clean by standing order following opening hours at the conclusion of each day,' said Mr McGrath.

'No doubt it is, McGrath. But there's the whole of the rest of the room. We shall have to put our scientific colleagues on to that.'

'But, sir, there must be literally hundreds of prints in a public place like that, and the chances of any of them ——'

'They won't find anything of the slightest use, of course. Now motive. McGrath, can you think of anybody who might want to get hold of Boris Karloff? I don't mean snaffle him in person, I mean have him snaffled.'

'Longbarrow Man', said Mr McGrath, 'is an archaeologically very rare and unique specimen, together with his jewellery and that. But he's not a very commercially valuable property. He would be only of interest to museums and to private collectors, who aren't in the habit of obtaining their exhibits in such a way. If you want my opinion, Colonel Manton, financial gain can be ruled out as a motive.'

'Which brings us to the coins. Could you sum up for Barrett's benefit?'

'Certainly, with pleasure. The Edward I penny, current value ——'

'Sum up, McGrath, sum up.'

'Yes, Colonel. It comes down to something of this, Constable. What we call the current value of the coins removed totals the sum of approximately sixty to seventy pounds. The current value of the coins remaining adds up to, here we are, round about sixty quid. Funny, isn't it, that? See, he missed the most valuable item in the entire collection, the tetragram of Syracuse. Only really old one we got, worth something like forty on its own. I can't see no sense in it.'

The colonel's prominent grey eyes were on Barrett, who said, 'Perhaps he just picked them out at random.'

'No, he took all the others that are worth anything to speak of, and left all the tripe, that is, the less intrinsically valuable pieces. Consistent.'

'Could he simply have missed the what-name? Not known about it or not recognized it?'

'The tetragram? No, Constable.' Mr McGrath shook his bottom-heavy head with a satisfied air. 'It has a card by it that says quite clear. No error possible. Very rare, it says. And it's a funny square-cut sort of shape. You couldn't miss it.'

'I can't see why he didn't go and pinch the lot, wouldn't have exactly weighed him down, just to be on the safe side. Can you, sir?'

'Clearly, for the same reason as that which led him not to take the tetragram.'

'Being what, sir?'

'I haven't the faintest idea. Now we mustn't take up any more of your time, McGrath. Let the police have a list of what's gone, would you? with any helpful details, any photographs you have of Boris Karloff's trinkets, and the rest of it. We'll be in touch. No, don't bother to see us down.'

'What chance is there of the stolen property being recovered, in your estimation, Colonel Manton?'

'Slender, McGrath. Good morning to you.'

Downstairs in the main hall, where there hung posters announcing cultural events in the area, the two officers of the law were approached by two other men. Going as much by his experience of films as of life, Barrett at once and correctly put them down as journalists of a lower stratum. The older one evidently knew the colonel and introduced the younger one. The few known facts of the case were very briefly divulged and some rendering of them set down on paper. Then the older journalist, who kept sniffing, said,

'I see you have a police guard on the museum room, Colonel.'

'It's customary.'

'Isn't that rather like locking the proverbial stable door?' asked the younger journalist, who kept scratching himself.

'To some, perhaps. To me it's much more like preventing silly asses from blundering in and destroying any traces the thief may have left.'

'Traces? You mean clues?'

'If you prefer.'

'Sorry, Colonel, but I can't help thinking you're, uh, you know, taking this business a bit sort of seriously.'

'All crime is serious.'

'Well, sure, but I can't help thinking a lot of our readers are going to think all this kerfuffle over an old skeleton being snatched is, you know, a bit of a joke.'

The colonel turned on him a face like Death at his most winning and informal. 'I don't care a fig what you can't help thinking your readers are going to think about anything under the sun, you funny old thing,' he grated suavely. 'Now you just take yourself and your buddy up those apples and pears'—he laid an arm round the waist of each journalist and urged them in the direction indicated—'and ask kind Mr McGrath to fill you full of local colour. Off you go, old beans—left-right, left-right, left-right, pick 'em up, pick 'em up. You know.'

Barrett was aware of a longing to smoke. All over the building, notices forbade him. When they were again alone, he looked rather dully at his superior, who smiled back at him.

'Yes, Barrett. Door-to-door inquiry both sides of the street up to St Stephen's Church, and then along left and right both sides as far as each corner. Was anybody walking home past the library last night and if so did he or she see or hear anything out of the ordinary. Nobody will have done, as I said earlier, but the motions have to be gone through.'

'You mean starting now, sir?' Barrett felt he had seriously misjudged Detective-Inspector Cox.

'Most certainly I don't mean starting now. Now is almost 1 p.m., and I wouldn't dream of sending a man on a job like that without a decent luncheon inside him. The very idea.'

In the passenger's seat of the Jaguar, Barrett said,

'Was he after Boris or the coins, sir?'

'Because?'

'Because he can't have wanted both. Different markets, wouldn't they be?'

'I should tell you that, according to McGrath, the necklet, which is the most valuable and what he called curious of all the stuff Boris was wearing, has no clasp and is fairly tight-fitting. They must have held the poor devil over a fire or something to join the ends. So you'd either have to pull his head off to get at the necklet, or take the whole of him somewhere and remove the thing at leisure.'

'Pair of pliers, sir?'

'Yes, but that would probably lower the value.'

'I thought we'd ruled out theft for gain.'

'McGrath has; I haven't. If our man did only want one or the other, which was it?'

'Boris. You wouldn't take him if all you wanted was the coins.'

'Nice simple thinking. And I can see a great deal in its favour. But there's absolutely nothing to suggest that he didn't want both, Karloff as well as coins, for some reason yet to emerge.'

'You're saying it will emerge?'

'I've no idea in the world, but something will. There's no question about that whatsoever—does a burglary as odd as this one strike you as belonging to the class of isolated occurrences? But a more immediate question, Barrett my lad, is as follows. Think carefully before you answer, and don't say you'll leave it to me. Are you a claret fan or a burgundy fan?'

III

View of a Victim

Peter Furneaux finished lathering his face with his father's shaving-brush and picked up his father's safety-razor. Tonight, Saturday, was the night of the tennis club's flannel dance. This strange expression, instead of meaning that flannel suits were compulsory, evidently just meant that evening dress was not. It was customary for club members to bring with them those of their older children who wanted, or in some cases could be compelled, to come along. Older children were children over fourteen, so that this was Peter's first chance to attend. He had needed no compulsion: on the contrary, he had looked forward to it almost without blinking since the fantastic stroke of destiny that had enabled him first to overtake, then to accompany, Daphne Hodgson on the last few hundred yards of their journeys home from school two days earlier. Daphne had been one down from the start, clearly disconcerted at being caught in public wearing her school uniform, with its grey felt hat secured by an elastic chin-strap, while he had felt comparatively dashing in his blazer and straw boater. It had been easy to make her part with the information that she would be at the dance, and possible to tell her airily that he might easily be there himself if nothing more worth while came up in the meantime.

Nothing had. Nothing could have, short of a date with Madeleine Carroll or Ginger Rogers. Peter had to suppress a physical tremor of excitement before setting to work with the razor. In one sense he had little need to use it at all, having shaved on the Wednesday of that week; but the Code of Dishonour was remarkably firm on the necessity of the utmost neatness and cleanliness at the outset of any degree of onslaught on chastity, even if it did reach that article rather late in its canon. Behind Peter, a bath was noisily filling from the verdigris-encrusted geyser, and into the former he soon stepped.

While he was wielding the Lifebuoy soap an idea struck him, none the less forceful for its utter lack of originality. He was about to get out of the bath to lock the door when a combination of other ideas made impact. As part of his undeclared, unremitting, and quite unavailing war on Peter's baser nature, Captain Furneaux had decreed that he should never lock that door 'in case somebody wanted something' (the shaving-mirror? the soap-rack?), and had been known to come stealing upstairs at times like this to check that his wish was observed. There would be better security later, in bed, and if—as Peter admitted to himself was very, very likely indeed—he should have failed to work his will on Daphne that evening, a form of consolation prize would be desirable. And to conserve one's ammunition, so to speak, surely made sense on any view of the matter, though it was true that here the Code had nothing to say. He must take it up with Forester on Monday.

He dressed himself in his favourite light-blue collar-attached shirt with blue-and-black-striped Tootal tie, the grey long trousers that had been under his mattress since the previous evening, and his school blazer. Daphne had seen the larger part of all this before, and recently, but only women worried about always wearing different things. Then, after putting a little Anzora on his hair—not too much, just to hold it in place—he went down to the sitting-room, where his father, in the leather armchair, was reading *The Times*.

'Can I have the wireless on, Dad?'

'What programme?'

'London Regional.'

'I mean what do you want to hear?'

'Geraldo.'

'Who?'

'Geraldo and his Gaucho Tango Orchestra.'

'And who might they be when they're at home?'

'Well, a gaucho's a South American cowboy.'

'If you imagine any of those customers have ever been nearer South America than Golders Green or Stepney, my lad, you've got another think coming.'

'It only means the style of what they play.'

'Mm. It's such a pity you don't care for any other sort of stuff.'

'I like jazz.'

'I don't mean that nigger row, I mean decent music. Elgar and Sullivan and Eric Coates.'

Peter did not say that he had never caught his father listening to the work of any of these three, indeed to any music at all apart from what might be broadcast during variety shows and the occasional feature or play. 'I like "The Grasshoppers' Dance" by Bucalossi.'

'Never heard of it. Well, old chap,'—Captain Furneaux's mood lightened quickly, as it did that one time out of four or so—'you switch on your cowboys and kick up hell's delight if that's what you fancy. I'm going to put a collar and tie on and then we can stroll along to the festivities. Have you had enough to eat?'

'Yes, thank you, Dad.'

'There'll be sandwiches and bridge rolls and things at the

dance if you start feeling peckish. I wish your mother would come back. I'm afraid I'm not much of a hand at anything more complicated than eggs and bacon.'

'That's all right, Dad.'

'Good. Well ... '

Left alone, Peter spent a short time wishing his aunt, delivered of an eight-pound boy the previous day, would get on her feet again and allow his mother to come home, but he had forgotten all about that side of life well before the wireless had warmed up and an announcer was announcing that here was Geraldo to say ... 'Good evening' was what Geraldo said, with another amiability or so thrown in, all in a manner that disagreeably recalled Captain Furneaux's views about the distance between London and South America, though Peter had forgotten all about that too by the time the Gaucho Tango Orchestra had struck up, not a tango, but a paso doble called 'El Relicario' by a certain Padilla. (The announcer had not announced this last detail: it had long been known to Peter by independent research.) Before the piece reached its second strain, he picked up and opened his copy of *The Aeroplane*—the twenty-fifth birthday number of that journal, which just went to show something or other that was slightly thrilling without being definable—not out of boredom with the music but to add to it, like having lemonade at the same time as ice-cream. How nice the nice things in life were, he thought. 'El Relicario' came to an end and now there followed a tango, 'Spider of the Night'. Soon Peter no longer really saw the opened magazine on his lap: his mind was gently invaded by images, most of them culled from reading and cinema-going, of sultry white courtyards hung with creepers and flowers, low-ceilinged candle-lit rooms, glasses of wine raised in a toast, and serious-looking black-haired girls in white dresses and long white gloves. One day he would have time to go there and see it all.

Peter's mood held up while he and his father walked along the riverside path in the direction of the dance. It was able to hold up partly because the weather had at last turned fine, a yellow evening sun gleamed along the water, the scrubby field on the further bank could for once be taken almost as a piece of countryside, and so on; partly because Captain Furneaux, suspecting, it seemed, no immediate threat to his welfare in what lay about him, was keeping his mouth shut. He had a way of keeping it shut that suggested dignified submission to final ruin, but that was not how he was going on now. In fact, on further inspection he had a contented, almost expectant air. Could it be that he was looking forward to the evening? Could he even perhaps be feeling excited? It seemed unlikely: grown-ups, especially men, seldom showed excitement in that sense, and this grown-up had no Daphne Hodgson to concentrate on. But that part of it was only a part of it; surely, no human being could not feel excited at the simple prospect of going to a dance? That was it, of course—the difference between feeling something and showing it. It must get like second nature with grown-ups to hide their excitement, and a good thing too, because a grown-up who was going to a dance with a Daphne Hodgson at it, *and who, being grown up, knew exactly what to do about her*, would just make a public exhibition of himself (to borrow one of Captain Furneaux's favourite phrases) if he were to show the excitement he would feel. Of course.

The river plunged into a culvert; the path acquired an asphalted, then a paved, surface and brick walls appeared on either side. Peter and his father came out into the High Street between the Express Dairy and the Dorchester

Dining Rooms (G. Bellini, prop.), and almost immediately opposite the office, formerly a small and mean shop, where Furneaux senior did his estate-agenting. Until they reached the end of the path, they had, as would have been usual even on a mid-week morning, seen no one; in the other direction, the path led only to Riverside Villas and, half a mile or so beyond them, to a country road that crossed the river—and, unless going to or coming from this end of the town, people having to do with the Villas would use the other road that started, or stopped, at the townward edge of the Meadow.

'Black satanic mill,' said Captain Furneaux, indicating his place of work. 'Form of legalized slavery. You enjoy your freedom while you've still got it, old boy.'

Luckily, this remark required no answer. If one had been demanded of him, Peter would have tried to express something of how fed up he had become at being handed this piece of typically grown-up balls once an hour or so by every male over the age of about eighteen. He would not have said his condition was unhappy, but by Jesus (a name taken only under dire provocation) it could hardly have been less free, short of them putting actual chains on you: everything you did or did not do was required or forbidden at the point of one gun or another. Your father won't hear of, if you want to please your mother you'll, boys are forbidden to, it is an offence to buy or sell, indulgence in this vile habit inevitably, duty as a Christian, by tomorrow morning, not until you're sixteen, get on with it, out of the question. I'm free, am I, Dad? Okay, get together all the money you'd have to spend on me in the next four or five years, book me a third-class passage to America or Hawaii or Paris, hand over the rest of the cash and write to the school saying I've left. Well, how do you mean I'm free, then?

Father and son paused at the kerb to let a bunch of three

cars go by in the direction of London: driving home after a day at the seaside, Peter guessed, spotting a child's bucket and spade through a back window. He wished there were a Furneaux car; he loved going anywhere, except to school, and he loved the seaside, a love which the annual fortnight at East Runton in Norfolk, where the water was cold even in August, did not fully satisfy. But a man with a handi-capped arm could not drive, which was lucky in one way, since the man in question was, as his son knew perfectly well, much too hard-up to afford a car anyhow.

On the far side of the road, and a couple of hundred yards along, was the King's Arms, and more importantly the hall at its rear which could be hired from the management for purposes like tonight's. Just as the pair were about to turn into the cobbled yard at the far end of which stood this hall, a new-looking, biscuit-coloured Morris Eight saloon that had been approaching veered suddenly to its left, crossed the pavement near enough in front of them to make each check in his stride, and drove up past the main body of the building.

'I might have known,' said Captain Furneaux a few seconds later, nodding his head towards the couple who had got out of the Morris: a rather short, slight, fair-haired man in a blue tweed jacket that went in at the waist, and a dark woman an inch or so taller wearing a long, dark-green dress and a wrap round her shoulders. 'Ill-bred little squirt.'

Peter thought his father seemed upset rather than angered by a not very narrow escape from injury. 'Who is he?'

'Hm. He is Christopher Inman, Esquire, and that is his lady. You must have seen him down at the club. He's an absolute rabbit—can't play for toffee.'

There was more, about jumped-up grocers, and push,

and gents' natty suitings, but Peter's ear had been caught by the sound of a piano playing—yes!—'Anything Goes' by Cole Porter: surely a good omen. Inside the hall, which had potted palms and curious blurred paintings round its walls, fourteen or fifteen couples were dancing a quick-step and a number, hard to estimate, of other people were sitting at tables, some chatting at a fair pace, not a few stolidly, perhaps here and there gloomily, watching the scene. On a stage at the far end was the band, over which Peter ran an expert glance. Besides the pianist, it consisted of a drummer with 'Bert Soper's Rhythm Boys' painted in gold on his bass drum, a *violinist* now adding his contribution, and a man who had a clarinet in his hand and was pretending to be fairly thoroughly carried away by what his three friends were up to. Rhythm Boys, indeed. There was no sign of a trumpet, which ruled out the prospect of any hot numbers worth the name. And there was equally nothing in the way of a guitar or piano-accordion, which meant no tangos. And a swift, if belated, check showed there was no Daphne to be seen either. Bloody hell. But it was early yet.

Captain Furneaux too had been looking round the company. 'Ah, there's Mr and Mrs Trevelyan. Might as well go over and join them, eh? just for a few minutes.'

'Yes, fine,' said Peter, a little surprised at, so to speak, having seen just now that Mrs Trevelyan was not Daphne without seeing that she was also Mrs Trevelyan.

Both the Trevelyans appeared pleased to see him and his father. Mrs Trevelyan was wearing a sort of fine net, which was pink, over a low-necked proper dress in blue; the total effect was mauve, or thereabouts. She had a string of pearls round her neck and more pearls in a pair of dangling earrings. There was a small bunch of pink roses, which might or might not have been real, in her black hair. What all this did was to make her look not only pretty but also rather important. Mr Trevelyan, a tubby man with mouse-coloured hair and a navy-blue serge suit, did not look at all important, nor could he be, seeing that he was a solicitor, the most awful and unnecessary occupation anybody (in Peter's view) could have, except (in one of his less closely reasoned, less fully conscious views) that of estate agent. But, solicitor or not, he behaved unimprovably now, getting the new arrivals seated and hurrying off to the refreshments table to fetch a pale ale and a Cydrax.

Before he returned, the Langdons had joined the group. Mrs Langdon was rather old, or looked it, with what people called a double chin, though the supplementary part of it actually consisted of throat or neck rather than chin; but she was all right really. Mr Langdon, tallish and with a full head of curly black hair, looked a certain amount younger. He wrote things for a living, and spent a lot of his time at home in order to do so, but the kind of things he wrote—odd paragraphs on almost everything of unimportance for the local paper—disqualified him, to Peter's constant regret, from being thinkable of as a writer. At the moment he was grinning, as if at the thought of a story he might tell any minute, and directed a cheery wink at Peter, whose spirits rose at once.

When the band had stopped for a rest, Mr Langdon said to him, 'Well, how's school?—if you can bring yourself to speak about it.'

'Oh, I think so. It's not too bad.'

'I say, do you really mean that? You are a lucky young shaver and no mistake. My schooldays were too bad from start to finish, I don't mind telling you. Of course, I didn't know then that everybody else's were too bad too in those days.' He nodded his head repeatedly and theatrically.

'Mine weren't,' said Mr Trevelyan. 'I was the school bully from the day I arrived, pretty near, so I had a lovely time.'

'I don't mean insensitive clods like you, Don; I'm talking about fellows cast in a finer mould, like me and all these novelists.'

'All what novelists?' Captain Furneaux sounded slightly impatient.

'Oh, everybody you pick up these days. They don't know how to begin except with little Percy having a bad time at school. Mind you, I sympathize deeply. And then I had the crass idiocy to do it all over again the other way round. A too-bad set of schooldays at the delivering as well as the receiving end.'

'I didn't know you'd been a master,' said Peter.

'Well, a teacher rather than a master—girls as well as boys. Six very inglorious years of it.'

Captain Furneaux asked, 'Where was this?'

'Of course, there were very great compensations, my young friend.' Mr Langdon, now Peter Lorre in voice and, to a remarkable degree, in face as well, laid a violently trembling hand on Peter Furneaux's arm. 'I have always much loved the beautiful leal children, to be with them and to be close to them. They are so sweet, so innocent, so— how shall I say?—so frajjle, and their leal necks are so very ... '

He went through exaggerated motions of throttling Peter, who played up by sticking his tongue out and rolling his eyes. There was a lot of laughter.

'That was that German one, wasn't it?' asked Mr Trevelyan.

'Yes, *M*—you remember. Strong meat for babes. Has anyone seen *The Secret Agent* yet? I have, in my capacity as film critic of the rag. John Gielgud and Robert Young as well as Lorre. There's a terrific scene in a chapel ... '

Mr Langdon did the scene in the chapel, and more besides. Everyone showed enjoyment, including this time his wife, who had struck Peter as not having cared for the *M* episode at all. Probably she had seen it done too many times before. After *The Secret Agent*, the Langdons went off to dance. This left vacant the chair next to Mrs Trevelyan. She smiled at Peter and tapped its seat, and he was there very soon.

'I suppose you'll be keeping a pretty close eye on the local girlhood tonight, Peter?'

It was amazing how she could get things so right without any effort that showed: no aren't-you-cute?-ness, no aren't-I-good-with-kids?-ness, just completely sensible. 'Well, that is sort of the idea, of course, but I haven't had much practice yet. And there's the age problem. One moment they're a child and the next they're older than you, than one, I mean, with boyfriends who are earning.'

She laughed, showing toothpaste-advert-standard teeth. 'You'll find the age problem has a way of going on coming up however old you are. Have you got any particular fancies?'

'I was thinking of Daphne Hodgson, but she's not here yet.'

'Oh yes, from over the way. Nice-looking girl.'

This was said so as to offer him, without any pressure, the chance of saying more about Daphne if he felt like it. He felt like it.

'I think so, but she's a bit, you know, heavy going.'

'What, you mean dull?'

'No, not really. I don't know her well enough to say. Not quite hostile. More high and mighty. Supercilious.'

'So that you get the impression she doesn't much like you.'

'That's it exactly. Not dislike, just doesn't much like.'

'Have you taken her out much?'

'Not at all. She won't come. I have asked her.'

'How many times?'

'Ooh: twice?'

'Not nearly enough, old boy. How many times have you met and talked to her?'

'Dozen.'

'Average length of conversation?'

'I don't know. Five or six minutes.'

'Then she doesn't not like you, that's for certain.'

'Some of the times she couldn't have got out of it.'

'Oh yes she could, believe me. How old is she?'

'Fifteen.'

'Peter.' Mrs Trevelyan lit a cork-tipped cigarette and sent him a serious dark-eyed stare. It did not have at all far to travel, because of the band and so on as well as them being confidential—good show. 'Growing up isn't any easier for girls than it is for boys. Daphne is just as unsure of herself as you are, but she hides it behind this sort of so-what and don't-know-what-you're-talking-about attitude.'

'Who told you that?'

'What?'

'She's always saying to me she doesn't know what I'm talking about.'

'If she does it again, tell her politely you'll put it another way.'

'A simpler way. If I can possibly manage to think of one by absolutely racking my brains.'

'No. Bad psychology with females. Keep that for your clever chums at school—don't you agree?'

'Good Lord,' said Peter, laughing. 'You're awfully, I don't know, it sounds silly, but you're awfully wise.'

'That's very nice of you, but I'm not really. I just remember things.'

'Well, I think it's more than that.'

At this point, Mr Trevelyan clinked one glass against another several times and asked humorously if he could have everybody's kind attention for a moment, obviously meaning just the attention of the group, which had now swelled to include an old codger and codgeress Peter had never seen before and a younger woman who might have been their idiot daughter and blinked all the time. When the kind attention was forthcoming, Mr Trevelyan said, in the same humorous way, only more loudly,

'Laid-ease and gentlemen, I have an announcement to make. In their infinite wisdom, the hierarchy of the branch of the legal profession which I have the honour to serve have seen fit to take me unto themselves. In short, I am to obtain the status of a partner, in recognition of which important event I give you a toast. To me!'

'Congratulations,' said Captain Furneaux as everybody stood up.

'Jolly well done!' said Mrs Langdon.

'To me!' said the codger.

'Not "to me", dear,' said the codgeress. 'It's not you we're drinking to.'

'All right, then: to him!'

'That's not very polite, is it, dear?'

Mr Trevelyan, who had a chubby face to go with his tubby body, broke into a laugh that, while he stayed relatively still, sounded as if he were being savagely shaken by the shoulders. Others also laughed, especially the idiot daughter. Peter wished he could take all grown-ups, except

Mrs Trevelyan and Mr Langdon and perhaps his parents, and drop them into the Mindanao Trench (maximum recorded depth 10,800 metres) which he had learnt about in geography earlier that week. He went on thinking this at intervals over the next hour, during which nothing happened whatsoever, unless you counted Mr Langdon dancing with Mrs Langdon again and Mr Trevelyan dancing with Mrs Trevelyan, and then Mr Langdon dancing with Mrs Trevelyan and Mr Trevelyan dancing with Mrs Langdon, and so on from that stage, and, to be fair, the band playing 'Body and Soul' and 'Saddle Your Blues to a Wild Mustang' but also, to be completely fair, 'Ciriciribin'.

Long after Peter had given up all hope of anything, the Hodgsons, four of them, suddenly appeared quite close at hand, taking up positions at a table directly across the dancefloor. With them, more particularly with Daphne and her brother Geoff, were a tall young man of about Geoff's age (eighteen) and a girl who was surely too much of a dud to be Geoff's: altogether a depressing sight. Whether or not the dud girl was the tall swine's sister, which was quite likely, it was quite unlikely that he was there just as Geoff's chum or she as Daphne's. He, Peter, had competition. After some minutes, the tall swine took the dud girl off in a slow foxtrot—perhaps they had after all turned up out of chummery of some kind. Anyway, the time had come to strike, or at least to tap gently. Peter muttered at what he judged was about the right pitch, got an encouraging wink from Mrs Trevelyan, who seemed to understand all the ins and outs, and set off round the floor into the jaws of embarrassment.

IV

Threats

'Good evening, Mrs Hodgson, how are you, Mr Hodgson?'
Politeness to potential victims' parents was enjoined by the
Code, but in this case Peter meant it too. Or fifty per cent
of it: however unpleasantly Daphne's mother's behaviour
(including stare, now turned on) could recall Daphne's,
her father was someone he had liked and admired almost
at first sight—not as funny as Mr Langdon, but somehow
more of a man.

Mr Hodgson justified these sentiments now by a hearty
greeting, an invitation to join the party and an order to
Geoff to find another chair. He was a little younger than
Peter's father and much bigger, a couple of inches over six
foot and solid with it, looking very much the policeman he
had been until a few years previously.

'Thank you, Mr Hodgson, I'd love to join you later, but
for now there's just one of you I'd like to join. I was
wondering'—Peter shifted his glance—'if you'd care to
dance, Daphne.' Pretty bloody neat, he thought.

'I've only just got here,' said Daphne.

'So you better make up for lost time,' said her father
bluffly. 'Get on your feet, girl.'

'Go on, Daph,' put in Geoff, no doubt anxious to evade
his chair-finding commission.

'All right, then.'

'Thank you very much is what a lady says when a
gentleman asks her for a dance,' said Mr Hodgson even
more bluffly.

Daphne said nothing more, but yielded to pressure to the extent of letting Peter lead her into the dance. Things in general were going well, standing in his favour, he thought, and swiftly ticked them off in his mind. He was probably not too bad a dancer for his age, being exceptionally quick on his feet, as his record in his House cricket XI (regular place second wicket down, highest score 41) suggested. The band was playing 'Georgia on my Mind', quite well really. Daphne, having been half coerced into leaving her seat, must be feeling at a disadvantage. And—this perhaps did not fit in very closely with the other items, but it fitted in somewhere all right—she did look remarkably assaultable in that peachy-pink shiny dress with the puffed sleeves and lowish front: much too old for her, as Captain Furneaux among others would have said in unintentional praise.

Quite soon, as they began fox-trotting, item three, the one about the disadvantage, turned out to apply in the opposite direction: Peter told himself he ought to have remembered how women feeling at a disadvantage ended up, or pretty well kicked off, by getting you at a disadvantage. Starting with her face, Daphne's whole frame took on a sulky woodenness which invaded item one, the one about his dancing abilities. He kept treading on her feet, and to say silently, in the spirit of Mrs Trevelyan's advice, that his partner was just as much putting her feet under his—well, it was all too theoretical to help.

'Sorry,' he said '— can we stop and start again?'

'Have we got to start again?'

'Oh, you mustn't give up so easily.' Peter tried to work in some of Mr Hodgson's bluffness. 'Just follow my lead. There's nothing to it if you've got any natural sense of rhythm.'

Either the bluffness, or the dig about sense of rhythm, or both, did it: Daphne, in her physical aspect at least, gave no more trouble for the time being. Peter even managed to force the front of him nearer the front of her; within an inch or two of it, in fact. Talk, on the other hand, failed to flourish. With a momentary lowering of spirits, he saw that he did not care at all what she thought about anything. The lights shone and dimmed and shone again, dozens of feet shuffled, there was a smell of face-powder, the man with the clarinet sang through a microphone that Georgia, Georgia, no peace he found, it was rather hot. Peter said,

'Jolly hot in here, isn't it?'

'Is it?'

'Well, I think it is.'

'Oh.' She produced her stare for emphasis.

'I thought we might go outside for a bit when this is over.'

'What for?'

At this precise point 'Georgia' ended. It was vital to distract Daphne's attention for the short interval before the next number began; she was more than capable of walking off the floor, on the argument that they had had their dance. Cued by her question, he made desperately sincere puzzlement first dawn, then come to high noon, on his face. Genuineness entered her habitual look of blank wonder. He had his audience, but, nearly doubled up by now with desperately sincere puzzlement, shoulders hunched, head lowered and rolling, and arms swaying from side to side like a gorilla's, he seemed to have reached some sort of limit. Would those flaming Rhythm Boys never get going? Then he had an idea: in fact, to make the sort of face characters in comic strips made when you could tell they had got an idea partly because they had IDEA! written above their heads. He made the face.

'What's the matter with you, you soppy date?'

The piano struck up what soon turned out to be 'The Touch of Your Lips', and she moved with him into the dance again. Objective reached—and more.

'I had an idea. At least, I thought of an answer to your question just now.'

'What question?'

'The one about going outside.'

'Eh? What about it?'

'I said I thought we could go outside for a bit, and you asked me what for.'

Daphne seemed too cross to speak, but she was still staring at him, indeed almost looking at him.

'Well, at first I couldn't think of an answer. As you probably gathered.'

'I thought you were going to be sick or something.'

'Oh no, it wasn't that. Anyway, then I thought of an answer.'

'Well?' she said very unwillingly.

Overjoyed at having extracted this prompting, Peter thinned his mouth and blinked his eyes rapidly in the way Steve (Mr Stephenson) at school had when, having outlined, say, the minor causes of the French Revolution, he was getting ready to tell the form what the main one had been. 'Because,' said Peter, putting spaces between the words, 'it's so hot in here.'

He realized in triumph that, for the first time in his dealings with Daphne and only about the fifth time with any girl, he had seized the initiative and held it for over a minute. But at once, perhaps because of the realizing, he felt that initiative begin to slip away. In a moment she would say her 'Oh' and he would have no comeback: he could not do desperately sincere puzzlement and its sequel again so soon, if ever, and he could think of no other thing like it that would not be too much like it.

'Oh,' said Daphne, and started to have her feet trodden on again. Peter stuck it out, through another violin solo, through a clear proof that the man with the clarinet was as bad at playing it as he was at singing, up to the end-of-set drum-roll and the dancers starting to clap (why did they do that?). But stick it out was all he managed to do. He had no heart for saying anything, let alone renewing his suggestion about going outside. He had been got at a disadvantage again.

Mr Hodgson looked from one to the other of the returning pair. 'How'd it go, son?'

'Oh ... all right.'

'Yeah, I know, no need to tell me. Just like ... ' Mr Hodgson started to look in his wife's direction, then changed his mind. 'Stay and have a glass of ginger pop or something. Geoff—glass of ginger pop. Here you are. Oh, now, this is ... '

Peter was introduced to the tall swine and dud girl, who looked respectively less swinish and more thoroughly dud seen close to. The ginger pop came and he tried to drink it as quickly as he could without looking rude. He was just finishing it when he caught sight of an elderly but good-looking man standing very upright at the edge of the floor and apparently watching the dancers. At once the man turned and saw him and kept his eyes on him. Peter looked away first, feeling slightly and obscurely troubled.

'Who's that gentleman in the dark suit?' he asked.

'Eh? Oh yeah. He's a gent all right. That's His Nibs

Colonel Manton. He thinks he's some sort of ruddy squire. Can't imagine why he's here tonight. You don't want to have nothing to do with him, not you.'

'Why not, Mr Hodgson?'

'Oh, I don't know, really. Funny sort of cove.' Mr Hodgson seemed to have lost all interest in the line of thought he had just started on. 'Have another ginger pop.'

'No thank you; I think I ought to be getting back.'

When he got back, after a grudging but perceptible farewell from Daphne that went some way towards saving the game, he found the party had changed a certain amount. The codger trio had (now thank we all our God) left it, and the Mr Inman he had had a glimpse of outside had joined it. Or semi-joined it, in the sense that he remained on his feet, moving about on them a little, in front of the table with the drinks on it. As Peter sat down, he was aware of tension in the group. Not that Mr Inman looked tense; now revealed as a rather effeminate figure with a pale but sweaty face, he was smiling amiably. He took in Peter's arrival, gazed for a moment, still smiling, at Mr Langdon, who returned the gaze with a blank expression, and seemed about to speak, but was forestalled.

'Cut along, old chap,' said Captain Furneaux with a very quick, worried glance at Peter. 'Best thing all round.'

'I will cut along old chap in approximately thirty seconds.' Mr Inman's voice was high and unexpectedly posh. 'I just have a thought to leave you with, Captain Furneaux. I ran into that bloke again the other day.'

'What *bloke*?'

'You know what *bloke*. The *bloke* who had the privilege of being a comrade-in-arms of yours in His Majesty's Royal Flying Corps during the late hostilities. There aren't many left of those, are there, your comrades-in-arms? No, all but a very few of them went down in a troopship when she was torpedoed in the Bay of Biscay—a fact which, let it be said, you have never endeavoured to conceal. Anyway, the *bloke* was positive he remembered you. Swore to it. Uncommon name, Furneaux. Pity. He had some very interesting ——'

'Clear off, Chris,' said Mr Trevelyan, who had risen from his chair.

'And don't *you* start feeling, Mr Tre-vel-y-an, that you are perfectly secure in your tasteful little semi-detached riverside residence. There are some items in your own situation that would not, as the saying goes, look well in the full light of day. So just you ... '

Mr Inman went on about watching steps and keeping civil tongues in heads while Mr Trevelyan walked slowly round the table towards him. Peter was struck by this demonstration, quite new in his experience, that real people could behave like people in films, and was rather enjoying it until he noticed that, while both Langdons seemed quite unmoved, unless by embarrassment, Mrs Trevelyan and his father were looking distinctly upset. The latter had turned pale, another novelty, and a disturbing one, so much so that Peter went over and stood at his side. Then, just as people in nearby groups began paying close attention, a woman in green, recognizable as Mrs Inman, came up and at once, with a single but earnest word of apology, led her unresisting husband away. Peter put his hand on his father's shoulder, and for a moment his father touched it with his own.

'Are you all right, Dad?'

'Yes, thank you, my dear old boy. Don't take any notice.'

'What was he talking about? I couldn't understand it. At least, I ——'

'He didn't know what he was saying himself. The fellow was completely pickled. Drunk. Now let's forget about it.'

Over the next half-hour Peter tried to do so, but at first he was nagged by the thought that, however pickled, Mr Inman had clearly known what he was saying. Then boredom, accompanied by a growing desire to go home, blotted out that thought. They had the spot prize and the eightsome reel, and somebody made a *speech*. Peter wished that he went to school in the town instead of in London, that his parents were more free and easy about who they let him get to know, that he had a brother or a sister. Should he have another go at Daphne? No, certainly not, far from it, not a celluloid cat's chance in hell, quite the contrary, tell that to the marines.

'May I have the pleasure of this dance, sir?' asked Mrs Trevelyan.

The walls of pale sticky toffee that enclosed Peter's universe collapsed at once. When they turned into each other's arms at the edge of the floor, even before they had stepped off together, he was very fully aware, first that Mrs Trevelyan's dress had no back to it, and secondly that the front of him was right up against the front of her, or the other way round. If this had started to happen with a girl of his own age, he would have considered he had gone a fair distance, but as things were it presumably did not count, in the same way as it would not count if a nurse ... no no no, it was nothing whatsoever to do with nurses. It did not count because however you chose to describe her she was not a girl and they were dancing, not, well, not doing anything other than dancing.

Perhaps the one thing helped the other, but they were certainly dancing with great ease. Peter knew after the first few seconds that Mrs Trevelyan's feet were never going to be under his; she had obviously had years of experience. He looked down at her pointed shiny mauve shoes.

'That was a funny business with Mr Inman,' he said to start them off.

'Funny's hardly the word.' Her voice was quite shrill.

'Well no, I just meant ——'

'He's a poisonous little swine.'

'I can't understand why he should have gone out of his way to be unpleasant like that.'

'There are some people who like doing just that, causing trouble for the fun of it. Anyway: how was the fair Daphne?'

'Pretty awful.' To say it made it feel much less awful straight away. 'I kept treading on her feet.'

'She'd better take dancing lessons unless she doesn't mind them going on being trodden on.'

'So had I.'

'You don't need them.' Mrs Trevelyan's dark-brown eyes looked into his with an effect of utter conviction; the movement brought their faces very close together. 'You're a natural dancer.'

'Oh, really, that's ... '

'I mean it. Anyway, how did the conversation go?'

'That was even worse. She didn't sort of react at all to anything I said, except with the so-what business. And it was only because her father ——'

'You mustn't let it put you off. Be interested in her. Or go on as if you were. Ask her about herself, what she wants to do when she leaves school. And—most important —listen to what she says.'

'I'll try, but that might be the hardest part.'

'You mustn't let her see it. Isn't this "Little Angeline"?'

'That's right.'

'They're not playing it very well, are they? Or am I wrong?'

'No, they're pretty lousy.'

'Who's good? I mean, you know a bit about dance music, don't you, Peter? Which are the good bands?'

'Well, all the ones you hear on the wireless are pretty good. Carroll Gibbons and the Savoy Hotel Orpheans, Maurice Winnick, Charlie Kunz from Casani's Club, George Scott-Wood and his Six Swingers. And then there are the Americans, like Paul Whiteman and Louis Armstrong, but you don't often get a chance to hear them.'

Peter had finished this in a hurry. Mrs Trevelyan had been looking at him again like the weight-guessing man, as she had done the previous Sunday.

'That's a lot of names to remember,' she said.

'You soon learn if you're really interested. I'm glad your husband's doing well in his business. You must be very pleased.'

'Oh, we are. Of course, it'll be a wrench in a way.'

'A wrench?'

'Yes, we'll be moving to North London as soon as we've got a house.'

Peter said, 'I see.' He wanted to cry.

'You mustn't ... You must come up and see us there. We're not going to vanish off the face of the earth.'

'It feels as if you are.'

'Well we're not: you'll see. Now let's concentrate on your dancing. You're good all right, but you ought to open out a bit, try more variations. What about a shot at the reverse turn?'

The reverse turn and things like that, and the straight-forward pleasure of dancing with someone as pretty as Mrs Trevelyan, took up so much of Peter's attention that for the moment he forgot his feeling that she was about to be taken out of his life just as he had started to like her tremendously. They talked hardly at all (not in the way he and Daphne had talked hardly at all) until almost the end of the third number, when Mrs Trevelyan said,

'This is a pretty tune.'

' "These Foolish Things".'

'Nice words, too.' After a pause, during which Peter was in very real and acute dread that she was going to sing some or indeed all of them, she added in a reflective but sensible tone, 'A telephone that rings, but who's to answer? Oh, how the ghost of you clings. Very well put, for this sort of song. I wonder if anybody special wrote it.'

Soon after that the tune and the set finished, and several things happened in a few seconds. The lights dimmed. Neither of the two moved away from the other. Peter saw what Mrs Trevelyan could not, a partial re-enactment of what had happened three-quarters of an hour earlier, with Mr Inman mouthing inaudibly and swaying about and, this time, Mr Hodgson looking up at him with hostility. Then Mrs Trevelyan shifted her position, masking Peter's view; she bent down a little, a couple of inches, obviously to kiss him; on instinct, he moved his head a fraction to offer his cheek; her fingers rested on his jaw and she kissed him on the mouth, not hard but not briskly, her lips shifting against his. At the same time the base of her stomach seemed to press against him.

'I'm not going away yet,' she said, so quietly that he could hardly hear.

His mind was suddenly overcrowded with questions, doubts, certainties, incredulities. As they stepped apart at last, his eye, which he had not dared to allow to meet hers, was caught by a movement twenty yards away:

Mr Hodgson, on his feet now, took a sudden step or two forward and hit Mr Inman under the chin, and, with a shock that could be felt as much as heard, Mr Inman fell across a table, dislodging several glasses, and on to the floor. After that there was plenty of excitement, but nothing to be seen for people hurrying to the spot. One of them, walking steadily rather than hurrying, was the man called Colonel Manton. Mrs Trevelyan took Peter's hand and drew him away towards the table where his father was.

V

The Afternoon in Question

The following Tuesday afternoon at about four-thirty, Peter was crossing the Meadow towards his front door. He carried a small cheap attaché-case; anyone who took a satchel to Blackfriars Grammar soon learned (by example only) not to. In the case were his homework books, copies of *The War of the Worlds* and *Carry on, Jeeves* from the form library, and that day's *Wizard*. He was full of happy anticipation of the rest of his day. The homework would take well under an hour: some general English—analyse the following sentences—and preparation of the next page and a bit of *L'Attaque du Moulin*, with the Congress of Vienna safely left to be swotted up on the train in the morning. The most important prospect was a visit to his particular friend, whose parents were going to a local whist-drive, which meant there would be plenty of time for ... (Here Peter's feelings went a little beyond happy anticipation for a moment.) Then, afterwards, home by paternal decree before ten o'clock, supper, the barest chance, depending on paternal mood, of a few minutes of Billy Cotton and his Band at 10.30 on the National Programme, and a torch-lit reading of Wells or Wodehouse or *Wizard* as finale. Bloody good.

He let himself into Montrose with his latch-key, dumped his case in the hall and entered the kitchen. Boiling the kettle on the gas-stove took no longer than cutting four slices of Hovis and spreading them with butter and Robinson's ginger marmalade. Five minutes later he was in one of the leather armchairs in the sitting-room, his back to the french windows that led to the garden and the river, a tray of tea and bread-and-marmalade on the pouffe at his side, the *Daily Mirror* open on his lap. There was a good twenty minutes to go before the London Zigeuner Orchestra, directed by Ernest Leggett, came on the air at 5.15. Peter read with interest that Jim and Amy Mollison had announced a new flight for the coming August, England–Australia–Fiji–Hawaii–U.S.A.–England, 27,000 miles in all—and with a different kind of interest that Dr Marie Stopes had published something called *Change of Life in Men and Women*: a New Book of Supreme Usefulness. He had no better an understanding than his form-mates of what the doctor actually did, except that she was to do with birth control, which put her in the right area straight away. Presumably this change of life was in the same area —but whereabouts? Change into what? Well, it could hardly be worth 6s. (postage 4d.) to find the answers.

Peter turned to the cricket news to find out how the Indian touring team were doing. Just then there came a couple of loud taps, bangs rather, on the glass of the french windows behind him. He turned and saw, standing on the narrow step, a man he did not at first recognize—leaning against the frame rather than standing, with one hand pressed to the head between eye and ear and the other uncertainly raised as if hesitating to knock again. Although he had no idea what might be in store, Peter was not yet alarmed. He unlocked and unbolted the windows to let in the man, who immediately lurched past him, overbalanced and fell face upwards on the bearskin rug; it was now clear that he was soaking wet from head to foot. Full of concern, Peter knelt by him and recognized him as the Mr Inman he had seen at the dance three days earlier. He saw too that

there was blood coming from a place on Mr Inman's
temple, not fast and not in great quantity, but quite enough
to show that he had had a more or less serious knock on the
head. His eyes were more than half open; nevertheless he
was snoring loudly. Peter decided at once that he could do
almost nothing for him unaided, and almost at once saw
what to do next. He went out on to the concreted strip of
backyard and called loudly for Mrs Trevelyan, on the
reasoning that at this time of day she was likely to be in
her kitchen or her sitting-room, both of which, like their
counterparts in Montrose, faced the back garden. If she
did not answer within five seconds, he would go round the
longer way to her front door and, if he failed there too,
down the row the other way to the Langdons at No. 11.
But as it was he got an answer almost at once. A door
opened beyond the high planking fence that, as with every
pair of villas, hid the back of the house from that of its
neighbour.

'What is it, Peter?'

'An accident. A man's been hurt.'

'I'll come straight away.'

Peter went back to the sitting-room and put a cushion
from the couch under Mr Inman's head. The snoring
stopped and the eyes, which had been looking nowhere in
particular, moved until they found Peter's face. In a blurred
voice, Mr Inman said, or seemed to say,

'Hallo. Hallo.'

'There's help on the way, Mr Inman.' Peter wondered
if he should do something about the blood, of which there
was more by now, but he had read that bleeding cleansed a
wound. 'I'll get a doctor.'

'Hallo. Heard something, turned round, hit me in the
head, fell down,' the man mumbled, then added more dis-

tinctly, though still very slowly, 'I had to tell him. I knew he wouldn't have liked it, but it was important. I had to be honest. A man has the right to know.'

'Don't talk,' said Peter. He knew that that was what you said to injured people; he knew too that he must somehow do as he had promised and fetch a doctor; nevertheless he felt he could not leave Mr Inman on his own.

'You're the Furneaux boy ... aren't you?'

'That's right, Mr Inman.'

'Tell him ... '

There were quick footsteps on the concrete, then in the room. Mrs Trevelyan, wearing a blue frock with a blue-and-white-checked apron over it, came and knelt beside Peter.

'My God, it's Chris Inman! How did it happen, Chris?'

'Hallo.' The voice had gone blurred again.

Mrs Trevelyan took a clean handkerchief from her apron pocket and put it on the place on Mr Inman's temple. 'Peter—go to the telephone and tell them it's an emergency call and they're to send an ambulance to this address as soon as possible.'

Out in the hall, Peter held the receiver to his ear, read the instructions on the base of the telephone and heard through the open doorway the odd noises coming from the sitting-room. Within ten seconds he had passed all the necessary information. When he had rung off, he found that the odd noises had stopped. Mr Inman was lying in exactly the same position on the rug as before, but he seemed more still, and had changed in some other way too. Mrs Trevelyan looked up towards Peter with an expression of total horror, frowning deeply, her mouth half-way open and turned down at the corners.

'He's not dead, is he?'

'I think so. We mustn't touch him. Fetch me that mirror.'

It was a small ornamental affair with paste flowers stuck on the top quarter of its surface to conceal the slogan 'Beer Is Best', and it remained unfogged after Mrs Trevelyan had held it close to Mr Inman's mouth and nose for half a minute or so. As much as anything, Peter felt incredulity: how could you die from being hit on the head if you could walk about in the meantime? He felt frightened too, but there were things to be done. He helped Mrs Trevelyan on to the couch, telephoned the police, telephoned his father. By that time the ambulance had arrived. The two attendants said they could do nothing until the police came. They too, in the persons of an inspector and a constable, were soon there. Captain Furneaux was only a couple of minutes behind them. He had, he said, run all the way from his office along the river-bank; certainly he was out of breath. He found his son in the kitchen with Mrs Trevelyan, who was sitting at the table with her head in her hands, and one of the ambulance men, who was pouring tea and asking Peter what he had learnt at school that day. Captain Furneaux embraced Peter and confusedly inquired what exactly had happened, and Peter told him as much as he knew without any confusion at all.

'What a dreadful thing. Who would do a thing like that? How do you feel, old boy? I don't know how you can be so calm. Marvellous—hundred per cent. But are you sure you're all right? How awful.'

'I think I'm all right now,' said Peter, sipping tea. 'You see, Dad, I didn't know him, just who he was, and I wasn't frightened when he came in and fell over, not till afterwards, I was more sorry for him, and I wasn't there when he died. It's much worse for ... ' He gestured slightly at Mrs Trevelyan.

His father began to move towards the silent, motionless figure, but checked himself. 'Yes. We must ... But imagine somebody bringing himself to ... I mean, it can't have been an accident, can it?'

The ambulance man shook his head. 'Foul play. All right, say he fell into the river and hit his head on something sharp. But the banks aren't high enough for him to be falling that hard, not on this reach they aren't. No, he got thumped and shoved in. I don't know how he got out again in that condition, but I dare say they'll be able to tell.'

'I think if nobody minds,' said Peter, 'I'll take Mrs Trevelyan home and stay with her till the doctor comes or Mr Trevelyan gets back. We'll only be next door if we're wanted.'

Nobody did mind. Mrs Trevelyan showed her agreement only by rising slowly to her feet and moving to the garden door with Peter at her side, but while they were walking down the cindered path, an underpopulated flower-bed on one side, a strip of lawn, too short for proper cricket, on the other, she took his arm and said,

'You're a brave boy, Peter. And intelligent as well. This was exactly the right thing to do, taking me home like this. I couldn't have moved a finger under my own steam.'

'Anybody could see that.'

'You were the only one who did, and you acted on it. Very grown-up.'

They had reached the bottom section of planking fence that hid all the riverside gardens from the view of passersby. He opened the gate in it and they walked the few yards of grassy path to the corresponding gate of the Trevelyans' garden. This Peter shut after them and made to turn away from.

'Please bolt it,' said Mrs Trevelyan in a conversational tone. 'Please see it's properly bolted.'

He did as he was told. It took him a little time, because the bolt was rather stiff—time enough to think that it was feminine of her (though understandable) to be afraid that another dying Mr Inman might be going to come up her garden path, and then to cancel that and decide that he himself was going to make jolly sure later that the Furneaux gate was bolted too before he went to his bedroom at the back of the house. In the interval, too, Mrs Trevelyan had changed her whole behaviour. Tears stood on her cheeks, her hands were clasped tightly together, and when she spoke her voice was harsh and halting, quite unlike the gentle fluency he was used to.

'Don't grow up too fast, Peter. When I was your age I couldn't wait to get out into the world, because I thought it was going to be so marvellous. Well it isn't. Things like ... they're happening every day. And it isn't fair. It isn't fair at all.'

She said the last words over her shoulder as she started running towards her kitchen door. He followed, but she was moving fast; blunted by a vague dread, his eye caught meaningless glimpses of an expanse of red-and-white-checked curtain, a crack in a pane, a trilby hat on a hall-stand, a Chinese table on which stood the wish-bowl half full of pebbles selected for their strange shape or colour, familiar to him from previous visits and therefore, it seemed, calming. Mrs Trevelyan had sat down on the edge of a chintz-covered chair with her thighs, arms, chest and face about as close together as possible. He rested his hand on her shoulder and was immediately possessed by a physical memory of her kiss so complete and intense that he felt he knew just what hallucinations were like. It made him wish it would happen again, happen now, be followed by more, by everything. But how dare he wish that so hard at this moment, wish it at all?—he snatched his hand away.

'Would you open the french windows?' she asked, her voice muffled. 'It's so hot in here.'

Peter was not aware of any undue heat, but again he did as he was told. Drawing the bolts and unfastening the lock brought such an unpleasant reminder of having done the same thing to let in dead Mr Inman by replicas of these windows that his calm, his confidence of having come relatively unshaken through a nasty ordeal, was not far from collapse. He wanted his mother there with her arms round him. But there was duty to be done. He took a deep breath and said,

'Can I get you anything, Mrs Trevelyan?'

'No thank you, Peter dear. I'll be all right now. You go back to your father. I'd rather be by myself for a while.'

'Are you sure?'

'Yes. Thank you for bringing me home.'

She held out a hand sideways without looking at him and he hesitantly gripped it, then, with a sense of slight and unlocatable disappointment, started to go out by way of the french windows before remembering about the bolt on the garden gate and leaving by the front door. He saw the ambulance and the police car and one or two other cars and a few people hanging about. In Montrose, a half-bald man in a brown suit was supervising another man who was taking photographs of Mr Inman. Also there was a doctor, who spoke cheerfully to Peter, made him swallow a pill and gave him another for later if he should find it hard to get to sleep. He did not need the second one: almost at once he began to feel very tired and, after being assured by his father that he need not go to school tomorrow, went up to bed and suddenly found it was the next morning and his mother was there with a cup of tea for him.

She stayed there, as close to him as possible, that is to say, for several hours, asking him how he felt, exclaiming what a shocking thing it was, telling him about his new cousin in order (she said) to take his mind off things, and asking him how he felt. At lunch, his father asked him the same question, and, on hearing that he felt all right, went on to ask him if he thought he could face a few minutes' talk with the police that afternoon, as tentatively arranged, it seemed, the previous evening. Peter said he thought he could. In fact, he at once started looking forward to it. A talk with the police would cancel out the lack of talk, earlier that day, with a small group of reporters; his mother, belying her look of blonde and ineffectual femininity, something she did all the time, had not only not let them in but had physically driven them from the doorstep. He felt that if he was going to be mixed up in a horrible murder he might at least be allowed any fun or fame that might be going.

At half-past two there was a knock at the front door. A policeman was standing on the doorstep. When, after a lengthy embrace with his mother, Peter went into the hall, he found his father there, wearing his bowler hat.

'There's no need for you to come too, Dad. I'll be all right, honestly.'

'It appears the gentlemen in blue would like me to present myself as well, for reasons best known to themselves.'

As they moved to the police car, a man in a raincoat asked if he could have a very brief word, and was told he could not. A man with a camera took a photograph. Good, thought Peter: he might get his name in the paper again, and this time, perhaps, in another version than Peter Firnaux, a 41-year-old schoolboy. After a few minutes, he said,

'This isn't the way to the police station.'

'We're not going there, son,' said the policeman. 'We're going to the Acting Chief Constable's house. He's taken charge of the case. It's not far.'

No more was said until the two were shown into the hall of what, to one of them at least, was a very grand house. The man in the brown suit, he who had been in charge of the photographing of Mr Inman, shook hands with them both and introduced himself as Detective-Constable Barrett. He said to Peter,

'I'm sorry to put you to this inconvenience, but of course we all want to catch this man, and we think you could help us a lot. You might be able to give us some very important clues. Just a few simple questions, not like an exam, because we're all on the same side, aren't we? If you'd care to wait here, sir ... '

Captain Furneaux sat down on the arm of a pink armchair, and Peter was taken into a huge room with wooden walls lined with books and, here and there, pictures with thick, very shiny glass over them. A man he recognized as Colonel Manton rose to his feet and smiled at him. Another man nodded to him from a sofa. This second, or third, man made Peter think of ferrets and rabbits, not because he particularly resembled either but because he had the sort of small body and small face that went with keeping the one animal in a pocket in readiness for going after the other. This was in spite of his smart grey suit, which only had the look of being hired for the day.

'So you're Peter Furneaux,' said the colonel, making it sound as if Peter Furneaux was somebody pretty important.

'Yes, sir.'

'Manton is my name. This is Detective-Inspector Cox. You've met Barrett here. Sit down, boy. It's not much use my telling you to make yourself at home, because you won't be able to do that. But I will tell you that we can stop this little talk at any time you choose. Understand?'

'Yes, sir.'

The colonel smiled again, or rather gave a mirthless grin, something Peter had often read about but had never had much serious hope of coming across in real life. It showed up his face as too bony for him to be actually good-looking, but he was distinguished-looking, though peculiar in some way too. Traces of the grin still showed round his mouth while Peter, on request, told in full detail what had happened between Mr Inman's first appearance at the french window and the arrival of the police. The detective-constable evidently took it all down in short-hand.

'Those things you say Inman said.' Colonel Manton fitted a cigarette into a knobbly wooden holder and lighted it. 'Are they verbatim?'

'I think so, sir. I was listening very carefully.'

'You read Latin, do you?'

'Yes, sir, a little, but I know the word anyway.'

'You've a good memory. It must be all those Latin verbs. What's the supine of *constituo*?'

'*Constitutum*, sir.'

'Are you sure?'

'Yes, sir.'

'You're the sort of witness a policeman dreams about, Master Furneaux,' said Colonel Manton, and added after a mildly odd pause, in which the man on the sofa grunted loudly, 'That's a French name, isn't it?'

'It was originally, but my father says our ancestors came to England in the fifteenth century.'

'No doubt they did. Now you say Inman kept saying Hallo. Are you certain that was what he said?'

'No, sir. It was as near as I could get. He wasn't talking very clearly.'

'Doesn't it strike you as an unexpected thing for a ... gravely injured man to say in the circumstances? Unhelpful? Uninformative?'

'It did at the time, sir, but not so much now.'

'What's made you change your mind?'

'He was very confused and I don't think he could see very well. He only just knew me—I mean he'd just seen me the once, last Saturday evening. He could have said Hallo out of puzzlement, or surprise, more than as a greeting.'

'Indeed. What do you think, Cox?'

'Possible, isn't it? Anything's possible.'

'Yes. Did you make any particular sense out of the other things he said?'

'No, sir,' said Peter.

'Right. Now as to the events at the dance on Saturday. I was there, as you know. Didn't I see some sort of altercation involving Inman and your father and some other people?'

'Well, there was one, sir.'

'Now then, boy, don't you come all literal-minded with me, or you'll earn yourself a smack-bottom.' Mirth of a sort entered the colonel's grin and left it again. 'What was said? As nearly verbatim as you can, if you please.'

Peter said what was said.

'And what effects did all that have on the other people?'

'Mr and Mrs Langdon didn't care for it, but that was all. My father and Mrs Trevelyan were upset. Mr Trevelyan was very angry. He'd have hit Mr Inman if Mrs Inman hadn't come along.'

'Could you make anything of what Inman said to your father?'

'Yes, sir, to a certain extent. My father's squadron was recalled from Mesopotamia in the last year of the war, in the April, because of General Ludendorff's offensive on the Western Front. But it never got there, as you heard. There were ——'

'Let's hear this from the boy's father, shall we, Colonel?' said Cox.

'Go on, please,' said the colonel to Peter.

'There were I think it was seven survivors altogether, including my father. Not from the ship—they were officers and men in the hospital who weren't fit to travel. My father had smashed himself up a couple of days before when his engine failed when he was coming in to land. His right arm's not much use even now.'

After another pause, the colonel asked, 'What type of aeroplane was it?' leaving Peter in no doubt that the question came from second thoughts.

'A Sopwith F.1 Camel, sir. My father can tell you all about that.'

'So he can. Let's get back to Trevelyan for a moment. You said he was very angry. There are lots of sorts of angry. Which sort was he? Wild? Raging? I couldn't see his face myself.'

'No, sir, quite the opposite. Dangerous-looking, but well under control.'

'I see. Have you got that, Barrett? All of it? Every little tiny scrap? Good. Good. I'm most grateful, Master Furneaux—you have helped us a great deal. Now you may care for something to read while you wait.'

The colonel went to his shelves and returned with a book called, it transpired, *The Hollow Man*.

'You might find this amusing. Be sure to leave it on the hall table when you depart. Thank you, and good afternoon.'

In the hall, the detective-constable said, 'Well done, youngster. You sit down here and have a good read. If you'd come this way, Captain Furneaux ... '

Son sent father a reassuring smile and wink, but the latter seemed not to notice as he moved into the inner room. Peter sat down in, not on, the pink armchair and opened *The Hollow Man*.

After a couple of minutes, he decided to look through it rather than to start reading it from the beginning. It would be awful to get all caught up in the story and then not be able to follow it through. So he glanced at stuff about coffins and salt-mines and masks before coming to a chapter in which the detective seemed to be haranguing his friends about murders in real life and in books as if they were the same. That was interesting.

... When A is murdered, and B and C are under strong suspicion, it is improbable that the innocent-looking D can be guilty. But he is. If G has a perfect alibi, sworn to at every point by every other letter in the alphabet, it is improbable that G can have committed the crime. But he has. When the detective picks up a fleck of coal-dust at the sea-shore, it is improbable that such an insignificant thing can have any importance. But it will ...

Bloody good, said Peter to himself, reading on. It was good even though you knew very little more about the story than that it was utterly different from the real story of what had happened to Mr Inman.

Dr Fell, his little eyes opened wide, was staring at the lamp, and his fist came slowly down on the table.

'Chimney!' he said. 'Chimney! Wow! I wonder if — ? Lord! Hadley, what an ass I've been!'

'What about the chimney?' asked the superintendent. 'We've proved the murderer couldn't have got out like that: getting up the chimney.'

'Yes, of course, but I didn't mean that. I begin to get a glimmer even if it may be a glimmer of moonshine. I must have another look at that chimney.'

Pettis chuckled, tapping the gold pencil on his notes. 'Anyhow,' he suggested, 'you may as well round out this discussion. I agree with the superintendent about one thing. You might do better to outline ways of tampering with doors, windows, or chimneys.'

On the point of turning back through the book to find out more about the chimney, Peter came back to himself and his situation with a start. By his pocket Ingersoll it was twenty minutes to four, which meant that his father had been under questioning for over half an hour. Just then, at the far end of the lofty hall, the front-door knocker sounded sharply. Somebody Peter took to be a servant appeared and let in somebody else, who turned out to be Mr Hodgson, and the plain-clothes constable also appeared briefly and asked him to wait a few minutes. Mr Hodgson, his footfalls loud on the wood-block floor, came strolling up. Peter got out of the pink armchair.

'No, sit down, sonny. Well, this is a funny sort of show and no error. You been in there?'

'Yes, Mr Hodgson.'

'Mm, you found him, didn't you? Rotten on you, that must have been. What did you make of His Nibs? Yeah, old Manton.'

'I thought he was rather nice. A bit sort of funny, though.'

'Oh, he's a scream, not half he isn't. Ruddy marvellous, the way these coppers' minds work, not that he's a real copper, so he's a dozen times worse. I take a swing at Chris Inman in public means I probably done him in. Makes real good sense, that, don't it? Your pa in there now, is he?'

'Yes. For quite some time.'

Peter would have liked to hear Mr Hodgson's comments on this piece of information, but at that point his father came out into the hall. He looked troubled in a way that, experience suggested, might mean either worry or anger. After giving Mr Hodgson a curt nod, one of his very curtest, in fact, he led the way out of the house in silence, a state he maintained throughout the journey home. He shook his head and gestured fiercely when Peter started to ask how he was. Outside the gate of Montrose, with the policeman driving away, he halted and seemed to relax a little.

'You were a long time with Colonel Manton, Dad.'

'Blighter's raving mad. Question after question after damn silly question. With that bald-headed little tick writing down everything I said.'

'What did they ask you about?'

'Oh, everything under the sun. What sort of man Christopher Inman was, had he got any enemies—I said he must have had at least one, which didn't go down at all well, let it be said—had I noticed any suspicious characters hanging about the place. And so on. A complete and utter waste of time from beginning to end. For all concerned.'

Peter knew his father was lying.

VI

The Weapon

'But could he have managed it in the time, there and back?' asked Barrett.

'That we must establish,' said Colonel Manton.

'I don't see how he could have done it anyway, sir, not with that arm.'

'Neither do I as yet. Patience, Barrett.'

'Anyway, he did come very clean about the crash, that is the non-crash.'

'He knew we could probably turn up the hospital records. Too probably. Or find that chum of Inman's. Now ——'

'I wonder he didn't go the whole hog and make out he'd been shot down, instead of just ——'

'*Barrett*, stop clouding the issue and get Hodgson in.'

'Have we got time, sir? We ought to go and see the river-bank and the car.'

Cox stirred his small frame. 'Knightley's there and it isn't going to rain and there's six hours of daylight left.'

'So do as you're told, you insubordinate rip.'

Barrett got Hodgson in and went back to his seat and note-pad.

'Sit down, Hodgson.'

'Mr Hodgson.'

'Good, I'm glad I have the name right. I'd be grateful if you'd tell me where you were between four-thirty and five yesterday afternoon.'

'All right. I was out Putney way. Upper Richmond Road.'

'What were you doing there?'

'I was on a case. Least I thought I was.'

'Explain.'

Sulkily and reluctantly, Hodgson said, 'Well, some-body rung me up, name of Evans, and asked me to a place called Number Two Hazel Drive just out of Putney. What for? I says, and he says too confidential to discuss over the phone. Well, I get a fair bit of that, and often as not it's a wasted journey, but I can't afford to turn 'em down. Where is it? I says. Off Upper Richmond Road, he says, north side, about five minutes' walk from Putney High Street going west. New houses, he says, only a couple finished. Well, off I go. On the way I takes a look at my street-plan, and I can't find no Hazel Drive where he said, but the plan's a couple of years old and he said new houses.

'Anyway, it's not there, Hazel Drive isn't, not where he said, and it's not anywhere as far along as Rocks Lane, nor it isn't on the south side of Upper Richmond Road as far back as Putney Hill. The last bit was just making double sure, because just before Rocks Lane I see a woman and ask her and she says she's positive there's no Hazel Drive anywhere round there, new houses or old houses. So, I headed back to the office fast as I could go, but it was all right when I got there, so I come home. That's it.'

Barrett had had to force himself to take down the second half of the foregoing. (His notation was not in fact short-hand, but a private system of abbreviated telegraphese adequate for purposes such as the present.) A name and a story were sounding in his mind. If they were doing so in Cox's too, Barrett would have been very surprised; if in the colonel's, he gave no sign, unless silence and immobility constituted one. He was standing up straight, hands behind back, and looking down at Hodgson, a brawny, or fleshy figure on the upright chair Barrett had picked the time before. Barrett felt he knew Hodgson's type: not much to him but a desire for advancement and authority, joined the Force in the hope of both, found the one slow and the other more regularly exerted on him than by him, left, set up on his own, indifferent success, general discontent, particular grudge against his former colleagues—not at all the kind of man to say the astonishing things he had just said.

Hodgson asked if he could smoke, was told he might, and started to. 'You'll want the times, I suppose. Left the office half-three or so. Got to where Hazel Drive wasn't, say four-twenty. Gave up looking after like fifteen minutes. Back the office half-five. Yeah, just about two hours. Plenty for you to play with.'

'Description of the woman, too, please,' said Cox.

'Don't know. Not young, not tall. I didn't notice. I was too het up, see?'

Barrett, on the green-and-black sofa at the far end from Cox, glanced at the colonel, who still did not speak or move. 'Het up about what?'

'Well, it was beginning to stink like mad. I didn't care for the bloke's voice first off. All deep and hoarse, like he was forcing it. Then, he doesn't give no Christian name or initials. Mister Evans. I don't pay much heed at the time— I reckon if there's two Evanses at Number Two Hazel Drive I can sort 'em out—but when there wasn't no Hazel bleeding Drive it all come back to me. The way I seen it, some sod had got me out of the way good and proper so he can have a go at my office. No cash to speak of, but lots of files and that. Confidential.'

'Where is your office exactly?'

'Just off Holborn, over one of them milk bars. Palmist on the same floor.'

'Could someone have broken in without being seen or heard?'

'Look, mate, I didn't draw no pictures, I just went there. Then I find everything's all right and I forget the whole thing. For about an hour and a half, till I get home and find Chris Inman's been done in and when, so I see where that puts me from your point of view.'

Barrett lighted a Craven A to give the colonel and Cox fair chances to speak and because he very much wanted one. He said, 'So you work alone ... '

'Oh no, I got ten assistants sitting round the office but they'll be no use without me when it comes to tackling a cove breaking in.'

' ... which means there were no witnesses to the phone call.'

'No. The palmist tart might have heard me leaving and coming back and leaving again, for what that's worth.'

'Any ideas on who might have wanted what out of your files?'

'No, but that don't apply, can't you see? Not now. Evans was fixing me up with no alibi for what happened to Chris Inman.'

'Interesting name, Evans,' said Colonel Manton. 'And a very good name. Better than Henry Smith. And much better than R. M. Qualtrough.'

'Who?' Hodgson seemed slightly puzzled.

'During your service with the police force, were you ever engaged on criminal investigation?'

Cox, at Barrett's side, gave a long, puffing sigh.

'No, nothing that grand,' Hodgson was saying. 'Copper on the beat, I was. Perishing bobby.'

'Does your present occupation bring you into contact with violent crime?'

'I do divorces mostly and the odd bit of blackmail. So, no.'

'Does murder, do murders interest you at all?'

'No more than the next man. Not until now, that is.'

'But you must remember the Wallace case. It was in all the newspapers over a period of four months. A bare five years ago.'

'What happened?'

The colonel glanced very briefly at Barrett. 'Wallace was an insurance agent in Manchester. One day, in front of witnesses, he was handed a telephone message from, ostensibly, a certain R. M. Qualtrough, whom Wallace said he'd never heard of. The message asked him to pay Qualtrough a call the following evening on business, though it didn't say what particular kind of business. The address given was in Menlove Gardens East. Wallace stated at his trial that he went to the Menlove Gardens area of the city, which was some way from his house, and found that Menlove Gardens East didn't exist, only Menlove Gardens West, North and South. When he got home, after over two hours' absence, his wife was in the sitting-room with her head battered in. Do you remember now, Hodgson?'

'Wasn't he meant to have stripped before he bashed her, so's not to get blood on his clothes?'

'That was one theory. Now there are at least two interesting differences between Wallace's story and yours. The prosecution's assumption was that he first committed the murder and then really and provably did go to the Menlove Gardens area. He asked the way of several people who testified to that effect. No more than was natural, said the defence. To make certain his presence was established, said the Crown. You only asked one person, whom you can't describe. Can you?'

'What of it?'

'In your case, the prosecution would contend that you never went to Putney at all.'

'Prosecution, eh? Come a long way a bit quick, haven't we?'

'How did you travel?' asked Cox.

'Bus. Underground. I don't take taxis when I'm not signed up on expenses.'

'Not even when you were in a hurry to get back to your office?'

'I would if I'd have seen one, but you don't get cabs looking for fares round Putney much.'

'Did you talk to anyone? Conductor or anyone?'

'No, I didn't, and what's this other interesting difference between Wallace's murder and mine, Colonel Manton?'

'The difference between Qualtrough and Evans. Qualtrough is a very uncommon name, originating in the Isle of Man. Now you could argue that geographical proximity would make it rather less uncommon in Liverpool than Southampton, for instance ... '

'Liverpool? You said Manchester just now.'

'Did I? Did I, Barrett?'

'Yes, sir, you did.'

'How frightfully careless of me: I can't think how I came to make that confusion. It was, in fact, Liverpool. Well: even there you could trace all the Qualtroughs very quickly and assure yourself that none was involved in the Wallace business. As was presumably done. That point, which was never brought up at the trial, is as good a proof of Wallace's innocence as could be wished for—I'm talking about inferential proof, not evidential. But now take Evans. A very common name, outside as well as inside Wales, without being at all suspiciously common. You could never trace all the Evanses who might have been in London or Liverpool or any other large city over a period of a day or two. Evans, in short, was just right for the job.'

'Meaning what?'

'Meaning that whoever devised this tale, whether you or another, had studied the Wallace case carefully and with profit.'

'Oh, terrific. I can feel the rope round my neck already.'

'I won't keep you much longer, Hodgson. I would just like to know the details of the altercation you had with Inman last Saturday night.'

'I don't want you to keep me any more than you do, Colonel Manton, so I tell you what, I'll let you have it from your side of the fence. Inman said I got pitched out of the Force for taking back-handers, that's bribes to you, and for beating a bloke in a cell one time. I say that's a lie, and you won't find nothing in my record about it. My record says I resigned, and I say so too. I can't prove I didn't resign to get out of the way of a corruption charge, but I haven't got to, have I? You'd have to prove I did, just as a preliminary to getting any sort of case into shape. Hopeless, my dear old soldier. You'll have to start looking somewhere else altogether if you want a motive for me. And make it a bit stronger while you're about it. What if I had taken a couple of back-handers nine years ago? Chris Inman tells Dick Langdon and Dick puts a bit in the local rag about it and I blows my brains out? Come off it.'

Red in the face, Hodgson got clumsily to his feet, marched out and banged the door behind him. Colonel Manton fluttered his eyelashes.

'Preliminary. A bad word. Very much not the sort of word for a dumb-ox, size-twelve-boots ex-bobby to use. I expect he found that pose was useful in his job, and then he started to grow into it. People do. It was bad luck on him that he got cross and let the mask slip. Until then I was believing every word he said. Would you care for some tea?'

Barrett said, 'Sir, I really think we should ——'

'Either we all have tea or you two watch me have mine.'

'Well, sir, in that case, thank you very much.'

The colonel nodded cynically and manipulated the bell-push. 'Yes, early and middle Hodgson wouldn't have taken the Wallace case in much, or, if he had, would never have considered adapting it for an alibi. But late-period Hodgson, the Hodgson we saw in that last minute or so, would be quite capable of it.'

'With what object?' asked Cox in a tone that verged on the peevish.

'Oh, to mislead us, to give us something irrelevant to think about. To make us decide he must be telling the truth because nobody would invent that story, or rather re-create it, least of all dumb-ox Hodgson.'

Barrett nodded. 'A sort of double bluff.'

'Well, loosely, yes. Loosely and partly. Don't forget he had to have an alibi of some sort. If he's telling the truth, of course, we're looking for a murderer who among other things is very interested in murders. I wonder if good Captain Furneaux fills that bill. Furneaux *fils* would know all right, but I must say I wouldn't enjoy asking him. Incidentally, Furneaux is a Channel Islands name rather than straight French, I think I'm right in saying, so *père* is given to romancing about the more remote as well as the more recent past. Let's go over that medical report again.'

Barrett, who had had momentary trouble sorting out feece and pear, produced the typewritten sheets from his document-case; the other two moved round and looked over his shoulder.

Christopher Inman (they reread) had died of an injury to the middle meningeal artery which had led to a sub-dural haemorrhage, which in turn had caused death by rapid cerebral compression. This had been the sole cause of death: there were no injuries or signs of interference elsewhere on the body, apart from a radiating fracture round the wound in the temporal bone—this, Barrett had estab-lished by a sly look at the dictionary, meant the bone of or at the temple. The blow had been struck with tremendous violence; judging by the position and direction of the thrust, it was the work of a tall right-handed man.

The nature of the weapon was difficult to determine. The brain had been penetrated by a metal spike of circular cross-section a quarter of an inch in diameter, the fracture caused by some much larger object, probably not of metal. No standard weapon suggested itself, nor, as far as the writer knew, was there any standard tool or similar object that could have been used as the weapon. Such an imple-ment, however, could have been devised in any number of ways. Although the injuries inflicted would normally have caused death within a few seconds, forensic pathology pro-vided sufficient parallel examples of subjects capable, for some minutes at least, of coherent speech, locomotion and, in one case, considerable physical exertion. There followed details of the deceased's general condition (excellent for his age, with no signs of disease), the contents of his alimentary canal (normal), and other lesser matters.

Tea, accompanied by buttered scones, mulberry jam, Garibaldi biscuits and a good deal of silverware and fine china, arrived while the trio were still considering the report. Making sure that his little finger stayed close to his others, Barrett sipped from a pink-and-yellow cup and said,

'Some minutes. I wonder how many minutes that is.'

'So do I,' said the colonel. 'We'll ask him when we have a better idea of Inman's movements after he was struck. If need be. It's the tall right-handed man that absolutely makes me want to fall into a deep refreshing sleep and snore like a hog.'

'Why?' asked Cox, chewing.

'Because, don't you see, it's madly dull. We've just been talking to a man without an alibi who's the only person in sight with the required physical qualifications.'

'Oh, that's dull, is it?'

'Well, isn't it? It would only not be dull if the blow turned out to have been struck by a small left-handed woman. I wonder if Mrs Trevelyan's left-handed. What fun if she were.'

Chewing more loudly than before, Cox picked up his cup and saucer and sauntered over to the bookshelves. Partly to annoy him further, Barrett said,

'We have been assuming Inman was struck hand to hand. Couldn't he have had something thrown at him?'

'By a professional darts-player with muscles like Samson,' said Cox with his back turned.

'Not necessarily thrown by hand,' pursued Barrett. 'Projected in some way. A bow and arrow, perhaps. Of course, they're rather inaccurate unless you're an expert.'

Cox slammed a volume back among its fellows. 'I'll tell you exactly how it was done. Mrs Trevelyan wanted to kill Inman because he knew she'd been a whore in the West End and was going to say so in the local paper. But she didn't want to stab him or poison him because that would have been dull, so she read up a lot of detective stories to find a madly undull way, as a result of which she stole a crossbow out of a museum and took it along when she met him by the river, and when he said, "What's that crossbow for, then?" she said, "To shoot you with, Chris." Or maybe she hid behind a bush and called out, "Keep still for a bit while I aim my crossbow at you, would you?" The only projectile that's fast and accurate enough to be any use on someone who isn't unconscious,' added Cox in a slightly less bitter tone than before, 'is a bullet out of a gun, and there isn't any gun.'

During this speech, Colonel Manton's face, turned towards Barrett and away from Cox, had been set in a silent and rather ghastly laugh. Now he said, 'Museum. Good point, Cox. So far we haven't found any possible way of linking the theft of Boris Karloff with the murder of Inman.'

'As the case stands at the moment,' said Barrett, 'Captain Furneaux's the favourite for the theft. He's the only one who spent that night on his own—I mean his wife was away. Of course, we can't rule out collusion between spouses, but until——'

'I see there must be a link.' Cox at this stage was trying to sound good-natured. 'Because it'd be so dull if there wasn't. I reckon old Furneaux was a regular customer of the Trevelyan dame when she was in trade, so he nicked the skeleton for her to use for target practice.'

To Barrett's relief, the telephone, on a davenport over towards the main window, started ringing. The colonel went and picked up the receiver, a half-eaten scone in his other hand.

'Manton. Yes, it is. Good afternoon. Yes. I see. Thank you most awfully. Goodbye to you.'

These few words were separated by long silences and

some vigorous note-taking. Finally, sighing and shaking his head, the colonel moved across and stood before the other two. He put his fingers into his trouser pockets and wagged his thumbs in a slow rhythm.

'That's a pity. That is a pity, gentlemen. The caller was one Greenfield. He completely bears out Trevelyan's story, having been with him in his office continuously from five-and-twenty minutes to four until shortly before five o'clock. You'll have to make sure Greenfield isn't Evans again, if you follow me, but of course he isn't.'

'Then Trevelyan's eliminated, sir,' said Barrett. 'Along with Langdon.'

'Yes yes yes, that's what I don't like. It restricts one in the most maddening way. Still, I suppose three suspects all without alibis during working hours would have been rather too much to hope for.'

'May I make a suggestion, sir?'

'By all means, Cox.'

'With the greatest respect'—it was probably the greatest respect Cox could summon, but it did not amount to very much—'I rather question your approach, sir. To me, it smacks of the amateur. My considered view is that a serious affair like this should be left in the hands of those who've been trained to do the job.'

'I've been trained to think, Cox,' said Colonel Manton with his grin. 'I naturally welcome your professional assistance.'

'I see. May I wash the jam off my hands?'

'The door opposite this one.' When Cox had gone, the colonel said, 'Barrett, is there anything to be said against Cox?'

'I, uh, don't know, sir.'

'Because there's nothing to be said for him.' There was

more work with the bell-push. 'Now, if you've quite finished feeding your funny old face, and I must say if that's your usual scale of tea it was jolly devoted of you to try to insist on going without it, we can be off and look at that river-bank.'

'Yes, sir. Sir, there was no need to warn me that you were going to say Manchester instead of Liverpool to Hodgson.'

'I know, I realized it the moment I'd done it, and I apologize.'

'Think nothing of it, sir.'

'Thank you. Right, come on, Barrett—the game's afoot!'

In the Jaguar, the colonel started sighing again. Presently he said,

'I'm depressed.'

When Cox did not speak, Barrett in the back seat said he was sorry to hear that.

'It's that weapon. What with the river and all the grass and greenery and so forth, and that's assuming he didn't take it away with him ... '

'They never found the weapon in the Wallace case either, sir.'

'No, and he got off on appeal. Didn't he? No, it's gone.'

This meant that, after they had driven a short distance out of the town, crossed the river, got out of the car, descended on to the riverside path and encountered the small group of county constabulary moving or standing here and there, Barrett was in two or so minds about how he felt (though Cox was clearly in just the one) when Inspector Knightley approached and said,

'It looks as though we've found the weapon, Colonel.'

'How ... incredibly clever of you, Inspector. May I see?'

'Certainly, sir.'

The inspector, a tall man with an appearance (and, in Barrett's view, an inner nature) of mild stupidity, signalled to Sergeant Duke, who hurried forward bearing an object that did look very much like a weapon; it was difficult, then at least, to see what else it could have been. The object, which Colonel Manton examined briefly before passing it on to Cox, was a rough wooden club three or four inches across at its fattest part and eight or nine inches long. Through that fattest part a stout nail had been driven in as far as it would go and crudely cemented in position. The whole thing was moist, indeed the wooden portion was to some extent saturated; net weight, perhaps two pounds.

'Hawkins found it not ten minutes ago, sir,' said the Inspector.

'Where exactly?'

'Far bank, sir, in the water, close in. Sort of held there, it was.'

'Well, that's a piece of luck and no mistake, eh, Cox? We must have a closer look at the place. But before we do that ... '

Some years earlier, not very discreditably long after a drunken tramp had, it was presumed, fallen into this stretch of water and drowned, the local council had had erected a white-painted wooden post-and-rail fence along the bank from the nearby bridge to the culvert under the main road. Closely followed by the two C.I.D. men and the Inspector, Colonel Manton made his way a few yards downstream to where a section of rail had parted from one of its attendant posts and now hung outwards at an angle. Upon brief examination and thought, Barrett concluded that the break had been made within the last day or so and that no very great force would have been needed in order to make it.

'Anything else, Knightley?'

'Just this, sir.'

With an air of leisurely triumph that could well have been irritating in somebody more intelligent, the inspector produced and handed over a pocket handkerchief, man's, good quality, white, slightly soiled, bearing, as was quickly seen, a legible laundry-mark.

'Any *signs of a struggle*, Knightley?' The rasp in the colonel's voice was as extreme as Barrett had ever heard it. He took the handkerchief along with the club when Cox passed them to him.

'Well, to my pair of eyes only the fence, sir. Ground's pretty hard. I'm no Sherlock Holmes, I leave that to these fellows here, but I couldn't find anything in the way of stuff trampled down, broken branches, any of that.'

'No. We've got enough. Quite enough. Now let's see the spot where your man came by that ... thing with the nail through it.'

The party crossed by the road bridge and entered a patch of thin woodland that straggled along beside the river. Fragments of cardboard and yellowed newspaper, a tin can and a bottle, part of a metal stove lay among tussocks of pale grass. Fifty yards from the bank a field of tulips began, thousands of them in regular rows that ended at a line of greenhouses along the main road to London. The air was almost still, but huge rolls of cloud, white picked out in grey, were sweeping diagonally across the sky.

'Right, show the colonel, Hawkins,' said Inspector Knightley. 'The exact place, mind.'

The constable stooped at the edge of the water, which

flowed by, rather fast and rather clean, not much more than eighteen inches beneath his feet. 'See that little bough curving out and round? Makes a kind of an eddy? Anything get caught in there, no reason why it should come out for a week or more. That club thing were floating there. I could see straight away it weren't no bit of branch, for the handle part were sawn off clean and poking above the water. So I found a bit of stick and I hoick it out.'

'Very observant of you, Hawkins. Good work.'

'Sir.'

'You can take your men away, Knightley; there's no more to be done here. You and they have behaved most efficiently. We'll go and see the car now and I'll be in touch with you by telephone.'

'I reckon you're even more depressed now, sir,' said Barrett to the colonel as they strolled away, Cox a little to their rear.

'I am.'

'Because now you're damn certain we'll never find the weapon.'

'Oh, for God's sake,' said Cox.

'Correct, Barrett. Before you give me your reasons, you agree the nail there will fit the hole in Inman's head?'

'Oh yes, sir. And the wooden part could have caused the fracture. And the laundry mark on the handkerchief'll be Inman's.'

'And the immersion of that club gadget in running water for twenty-four hours would have washed away, or couldn't be proved not to have washed away, all traces of blood, skin, hair and so on.'

'Give me strength,' said Cox, unregarded by the other two.

'Yes, sir. Now we'll say I'm the murderer. I get Inman

to meet me at a deserted spot—he comes although he knows I've got something against him, and he leaves his car well down the road, away from where he's going to meet me. While he's waiting, he blows his nose and chucks the handkerchief on the ground. I've been to a lot of trouble to make a club with a spike on it to hit him with, when a knife would have served as well or better, and I hit him in the skull, when the throat, say, would have been easier. Now either I'm Hodgson, what you called late-period Hodgson, or I'm Evans, so either way I'm an intelligent man. So I break the fence and push Inman into the river—what for? —and then, instead of taking the weapon away with me and dropping it out of a train window or something, I throw it into the river just where an ordinary copper'll find it.'

'Hell's bells and buckets of blood,' said Cox. 'He hit him in the skull because in the struggle that was the only place he could get at, and he thought someone was coming so he heaved the club into the water, and he shoved Inman in too to make sure ——'

'But no one was coming, else they'd have seen ——'

'I said he thought. Jesus. The trouble with you, Barrett, you read too much. And you think too much.'

Having said this, Cox dropped further behind. Barrett's speech seemed to have alleviated the colonel's depression; at any rate, when he spoke it was with something not far removed from his normal peevish jocularity.

'What you said was all very fine and large, Barrett, but you seem to forget that I'm the one who's supposed to work everything out in that style. You're simply the ——'

'But, Colonel, this is marvellous? You mean that kind of thing?'

'Not another *word*, Barrett.'

They had reached Inman's Morris, pulled on to a chalky

verge round a corner from the bridge. The constable on guard saluted Colonel Manton and, on being told he could now leave, left.

'You'll have to go over it. Door-handles, steering-wheel, gear lever, handbrake, all that.'

'Would that be for finger-prints, sir?' Cox spoke as of an ephemeral fad.

'Yes, Cox, it would. You won't find anything. No, that's not quite true. You'll almost certainly find nothing but Inman's and Mrs Inman's and their garage-man's, but you might conceivably find none at all. It would be just about worth knowing if that were the case. Take that bogus bludgeon down to the doctor before he shuts up shop. Then, tomorrow, after the inquest, I want a full report on progress to date, including the Furneaux possibility, Inman's movements, Mrs Inman, the whole thing. You needn't bother to have it typewritten.'

'That's a lot of work in the time, Colonel.'

'A sufficient amount. And *no*, Cox, and *no*, Barrett, we are not going to call in Scotland Yard. You know very well we never do that. By which I mean ... If we need more strength I'll get Binkie Aston of Surrey to lend us someone. Aston was on the staff of my division in France for a time. But I'm confident that our county C.I.D. will prove adequate to all tasks laid upon it. Now get to work.'

The clouds had parted a minute before and the three stood beside the empty Morris in strong sunlight. Barrett glanced down, as he had a dozen times already, at the spiked club in his hand. Now, in the brightness, his sharp eyes picked out something they had missed before.

'My God! Look, sir!'

The colonel brought out elongated pince-nez and peered through them. 'I still can't see.'

'There are some tiny cracks round just there, where the nail comes out, where he split the wood driving it in, I reckon. Well, there's a hair caught in one of them.'

'A fair hair. It must be.'

'That's right, sir. Inman's.'

'So we haven't started,' said Colonel Manton, folding his arms and glancing sidelong at Barrett. 'We know nothing at all.'

'Speak for yourselves,' said Cox.

VII

Moments of Delight

The next day, Thursday, Peter went to tea with his particular friend, whose name was Reg except according to his mother: she called him Reggie. Peter could not help noticing (as one neither blind nor barmy) that she gave him a funny look when she let him in, and also that, in the way of grown-ups, she thought he could not possibly notice because he was not grown-up himself. But, after a day at school, he was pretty well used to funny looks. Not that they were all he had had: a group of his friends had said what a jolly rotten experience it must have been before making him tell them all the details, and Mr Taylor had taken him aside at the beginning of break and said there was probably nothing he could do to help, but if there should be anything, large or small, then Peter must not hesitate to let him know. He had been so decent that it had been very difficult not to start crying.

Reg's mother gave him more funny looks while the three of them sat at the tea-table, though she kept off the actual subject as utterly as if it had been sex. It was, as usual, a tip-top tea, with two kinds of jam, chocolate éclairs and cream horns. When not a great deal of jam and nothing whatever of anything else was left, the boys swapped respectable stories about their schools for the time it took Reg's mother to smoke a De Reszke Minor. Then Reg asked if they could get down and was told they could. Peter got a final funny look as they went out.

Up in his bedroom, Reg stood on a chair to bring down a packet of Turban from the top of his wardrobe. At $2\frac{1}{2}d$. for twenty, these smokes were regarded by everyone as the best value in the market, but they were hard to come by. Only one shop in the town sold them, and the man in it was annoyingly keen on the law about no tobacco for under-sixteens. Reg, though in fact nearly a year younger, could pass for sixteen; Peter could not, and had to stretch an already tight budget by getting Weights or Woodbines out of slot-machines at $4d$. for ten. Occasionally Reg remembered his constant promise to get Turban on Peter's behalf, but not this time.

Reg's father, who was a buyer in Jay's at Oxford Circus, earned more money than Peter's father. Signs of this lay all round the room, especially on the top of the chest of drawers, where a couple of hundred lead soldiers (just a contingent of the total standing army) marched, rode and served artillery: Scots Greys, Royal Dragoons, 16th/5th Lancers, Coldstream Guards, Territorials, British infantry in gas-masks. In particular, there was a whole section—three guns—of long-barrelled naval 4·7s, where Peter could only afford a couple of 18-pounders. But Reg was good about this difference in their circumstances, never referring to it, handing on books and comics he would say he had finished with, leaving half-full packets of Turban behind when he came to tea at Peter's and not asking for them back.

Each lit up a Turban now at the open window, an outlet for the smoke and, in emergency, the cigarette itself.

'Have you heard the one about the blind man in the nudist colony?' asked Reg.

'No,' said Peter, though he had.

'He couldn't see, so he just felt his way about.'

Peter laughed genuinely, out of not amusement but

pleasure at being brought on to the right ground. 'I haven't heard any for ages.'

'Have you heard the one about the young man of Chislehurst?'

'No.' This was true.

'There was a young man of Chislehurst, who when he peed had to whistle first. One hot day in June he forgot the tune, da da da da da da da da da.'

'How do you mean, da da da da da da da da da?'

'Well, I suppose he broke his bladder or something.'

'But there ought to be a proper last line saying so.'

'You make it up, then.' Reg looked bored, then animated again. 'Hey, I had a super one in the bath last night. The old soapy-hand method. Do you do that much?'

'A bit.'

'Do you think it does you any harm, you know, doing it?'

'I shouldn't think so. You know Forester?'

'Yes,' said Reg, meaning he well knew who Forester was.

'He says wasting time doesn't do you any harm as long as you don't take it too seriously.'

'Hey, that's pretty good. As far as I'm concerned, sometimes I take it seriously and sometimes I don't. I always think it's marvellous it being so easy. You know, nothing to learn or practise.'

'Same here. It's like a free strawberry sundae really.'

This high praise seemed lost on Reg, who said, 'I don't half feel like it now,' and massaged himself briefly.

'So do I, but we can't yet. Let's have a record.'

With the cigarette-ends flung as far as possible out of the window, Reg went and wound up his H.M.V. table model and changed the Extra Loud steel needle—the only sort he ever used. Peter turned through the piles of ten-inch records in their stout cardboard covers. When Reg had finished with handle and sound-box, he came and looked over Peter's shoulder.

'What about this one?' Reg pulled out and put on the turntable a record with a light-blue label. ' "Hors d'Œuvres". Ambrose and his Orchestra.'

The needle clumped into the first or so groove. Both, as always, listened with total concentration throughout, tapping their feet but otherwise not moving.

'Bloody good,' said Peter when it was over.

'Shit hot.'

'Terrific piano. What does it mean, the title?'

'It's what you have for your first course when you have dinner in an hotel. Sardines and tomatoes and stuff.'

'Oh.'

'Now you choose one.'

Peter chose a Rex record, a tango called 'Moonlight Kisses' played by Troise and his Mandoliers. He and Reg had recently seen and heard this organization performing as part of the stage-show at the local Gaumont, but their acquaintance with its work went far beyond that. The music began. Almost at once, an accordion played a fast ascending run that put Peter in mind of a bird taking flight and made him want to shiver. Then, after mandolines and accordion had shared the verse, Don Carlos entered with the vocal refrain. (Peter was well aware that Don Carlos doubled as the Vagabond Lover on the B.B.C. and was also, or perhaps really, called Cavan O'Connor, but that did not make him any the less Don Carlos.)

> 'Love ...
> Bring back those moments of delight,
> The tender passion of that night
> Of moonlight kisses ...'

And so on. Peter knew that the words were quite probably soppy, but he did not want to decide they were, nor did he feel them to be so. It would be nice to have somebody real in your mind, some actual person you could think of as having to do, however vaguely, with moments of delight and tender passion. Daphne, he saw with some pain, and then with some boredom, would never play any such part for him. But ... Mrs Trevelyan ... Peter's thoughts turned abruptly aside from that idea. He was a fool; what had happened at the end of that last dance the previous Saturday had meant nothing; it was all his imagination; she had just been being affectionate; he must forget it.

Don Carlos came in again at the end:

> '*Love ...*
> *That moon above need never shine*
> *Until your lips are pressed to mine*
> *In moonlight kisses.*'

The band stopped on a chord that made you want another chord after it, but that was how all the best tangos ended. Reg took the tone-arm off the record, and immediately his mother, with what was, for her, very bad timing (she normally made her presence felt in mid-record, mid-cigarette, or mid-something-else much more vital), called her version of his name from the floor below. He went to the door and opened it.

'Yes, Mummy?'

'I'm just off to fetch Daddy.'

'Right-oh, Mummy.'

Reg shut the door. By careful research, backed up by regular checks, he had established beyond doubt that the minimum time it took his mother to go out to the car, take it to the station, collect his father and return home was twenty-two minutes. Because she seldom left the house without coming back for something, the first four of these were agreed not to count; the two boys used them up by going to the lavatory one after the other. That afternoon they heard the car drive out of the garage and off up the road with no prolonged delay.

'Right,' said Reg, looking at his wrist-watch and unclasping his belt.

It was his turn to go first and, fair-minded as ever, he made no bones about going first. Going second was better because you were still in the mood, or more so, less good because the one who had been first was not, or not so much, but on balance it was considerably better. Even so, when they were fit to be seen again and, according to ritual, had lit another Turban each, Peter felt a little let down, though not out of any fault or defect on his friend's part. It was so soon over (all that happened when they had longer was more records and then a second go), so much less than you had been sure it was going to be. But there seemed no way of making it count more. Reg was as presentable a boy as any Peter remembered seeing, but he did not want to be kissed by him or undressed with him—especially not, of course, at moments like this.

'How's Betty?' asked Peter, referring to the family's maidservant.

'All right. If only she was about six and a quarter per cent better. Just that much. Look, she's seventeen, she must know what it's about. I'm darn sure she wouldn't scream the place down if I had a go at her. I keep thinking I will when I'm playing with my John Thomas. In fact, I tell you frankly, quite a few times when we've been alone in the house I've come up here and worked myself up, let it just go down and rushed off to where she is in the kitchen or somewhere, and then I sort of notice her face and I feel as though I've just had one. Funny how it all gets so different, one minute to the next, isn't it?'

'I know,' said Peter, adding after a pause, 'Do you talk to her at all?'

For some momentarily mysterious reason, this query did not seem to please Reg. He looked physically uncomfortable, adjusting his shirt-collar and even blowing his nose, an almost unheard-of action in him. After a silence, he said,

'She knows some of the other maids round here, you see.'

'What about it?'

'Well ... one of them's the girl-friend of some policeman. Constable, I suppose he is.'

'Yeah?'

'Well, according to what Betty was telling me last night, this copper thinks your pa was mixed up in this murder down round your place. At least the copper's bosses think so, the inspectors or whatever they are.'

Hardly a day went by on which Peter did not read of somebody going cold with fear. What was meant, he saw now, was that your scalp went so hot that the back of your neck and the tops of your shoulders felt cold by comparison. He said,

'What do they mean, mixed up in it? They mean they think he did it?'

'Mixed up in it was what Betty said.'

'But he couldn't have done it: he was in his office all the time. I spoke to him on the phone.'

'You know these coppers.'

'He couldn't have done a thing like that, not my pa.'

'Course he couldn't. I just thought I ought to tell you.'

'He couldn't have.'

Reg went over to the gramophone, but did not touch it or any of the records. 'The inquest was today.'

'How do you know?'

'My pa said. Were you there? You weren't, were you?'

'They said I needn't. They took a statement for them to read out.'

'Sorry, Pete, I wish I hadn't told you.'

So did Peter, very strongly, but only in a way: it was better to be forewarned. As, not long afterwards, he walked home, he tried to breathe normally and to think. Character of the accused. Is your father a hot-tempered man? We want the truth, now. He can be, sir. Has he ever struck you? Yes, sir. Frequently? Fairly frequently, sir. Has he ever, to your knowledge, struck your mother? No, sir. Is he the sort of man to bear a grudge? No, sir. Once he threw a book of mine into the fire and afterwards he was very sorry and asked me what it was called and got me another copy. No doubt, but what we want to know is, is he capable, psychologically speaking, of having done this dastardly deed? Well, he might conceivably strike out at a man in a fit of blind rage without intending to kill him and then find to his horror that he had done so. In that unlikely event, sir, he would be filled with remorse. Would he not, as many men would, endeavour to conceal his guilt? No, sir, he would give himself up to the proper authorities as soon as was humanly possible. That is your opinion. True, but an opinion based on long and close —— I repeat that it is your opinion.

This was starting to be almost fun, but he could not stave off indefinitely the question whether whatever his father had done in the R.F.C. was so bad that a man as sane as he would have felt compelled to kill Mr Inman as the only

way of keeping the secret. Walking through the town under
a mixed grey sky on the point of rain, Peter felt physically
frightened, as though the fat red chimney-pot above the
Fifty-Shilling Tailors were about to fall on him. He realized
he was hurrying and forced himself to walk at an ordinary
pace. The thing was to look at it all quite dispassionately,
like a story. Desertion in the face of the enemy; but they
shot you for that, and in any case his father would never ...
No, that was no argument, because if he could kill someone
he was not as he had always seemed, and if he were not that
he could quite well have deserted. But anyway you got shot
for it. Desertion not in the face of the enemy. Stealing some
money, the money belonging to the officers' mess. Raping a
native woman—but surely ... No.

Suddenly, Peter's fear left him. Whatever his father had
done must have been found out by the authorities and put
on record, because if it had not been then it was all just a
rumour, hearsay, one man's word against another's. And if
it had been, then, like any other man with a past, he would
surely have changed his name, all the more surely for its
being, as Mr Inman had pointed out, such an uncommon
one. So the R.F.C. business must have been quite trivial.
Everything was all right—all right even without going into
the alibi question. And his father obviously had an alibi.

Peter knew, from his occasional visits to the office as well
as from a great deal of conversation, that there was a girl
assistant there, referred to as the dogsbody, who was
always round the place typing and answering the telephone.
That afternoon up at Colonel Manton's house, he and the
other detectives must have been asking his father about Mr
Inman's sex-life, was he one for the women and so could
there be any jealous husbands or angry fiancés about. That
was the reason for those lies afterwards. Something like

that. By the way, it would be nice when (and, you could pretty well bloody well add, if) his parents let him out of his continuing state of official belief in storks and gooseberry bushes and doctors' black bags as means of arrival in this world.

He was thinking quite happily about the real means, or rather about the exercise that led to it, when he opened the front door of Montrose with his latchkey and put his attaché-case down next to the hallstand, with the intention of getting a glass of milk from the kitchen before starting on his homework. For no reason he could have named, his glance fell on the photograph of his father in R.F.C. uniform and—it struck Peter as never before—in a rather studied, thoughtful pose, hand cupped round chin. The sight recalled to him the last time he had noticed this photograph, something like ten days earlier, just after its subject had so uncharacteristically, and in such apparent distress, talked about the doings of a murderess and a murderer. Doubt and anxiety revisited Peter, and at that exact moment he heard a movement from the sitting-room, the sound of someone shutting the french window there.

Peter had (unconsideringly) expected to return to an empty house, his mother off to see that all continued to be well with her sister and new nephew, his father still at work or just starting on his way home. This expectation was part of the reason why, on hearing the sound from the sitting-room, Peter thought, very vividly indeed, of Mr Inman lurching into that room sopping wet and with a hole in his head. He, Peter, backed a little unsteadily towards the door by which he had just entered. Then he heard a familiar voice saying, in an unfamiliar tone,

'Who's there? Is that you, Peter old boy?'

'Yes. Yes, Dad.'

He and his father went into a prolonged hug somewhere near the threshold of the sitting-room.

'Are you all right? I hope I didn't startle you. Did I? I was taking a turn in the garden. I got a bit of a headache and I thought to hell with it, let's shut the damn place up for once in a way and get on home. Which, as you can well see, I duly proceeded to do. How was old Reg? Nice lad, that. Are you sure you're all right? Well, I don't know about you, but I could do with a cup of real old sergeant-major's tea. Stand your spoon up in it.'

By now they had moved into the kitchen. Peter's own fear had abated, but he still felt disquiet at the fear that had shown in his father's voice when he first spoke. What was there to be afraid of? Or was he just nervy, strung up? But why should he be? Business worries? But could anything in estate-agenting be important enough to make anybody worry? Captain Furneaux, making the tea, talked about estate-agenting, but not in such a style as to indicate or cause worry. Indeed the effect on Peter was that of a mighty sedative, as nearly always; not as quite always, because just now and then the realization that one day he himself was going to have to rent or buy a house of some sort would fill him with dismay and despair, like the thought of going over the top at Ypres or the Somme without any prospect of a medal.

Peter's father poured the tea and took two digestive biscuits out of the tin with the Japanese ladies painted on it. Peter took two as well, not because he liked them, in fact he could never decide whether they revolted him more than they bored him or the other way on, but because grown-ups liked them, ate them, at least, and the nearer you got to being grown-up the plainer you could see that you needed all the practice for it you could come by. As he chewed and pretended to listen, he was trying to think of a way of putting his mind at rest about his father's alibi without giving it away that that was what he was doing. Then there came a reference to the dogsbody.

'Did she really? Well, it was a jolly good thing she was with you in the office that day.'

Captain Furneaux did not ask what day or what part of it. 'A jolly good thing?'

'So's the police know you couldn't have killed Mr Inman.'

'They know no such thing, old boy.'

VIII

The Second Strike

'Listen, you'd better have the facts before you get them all jumbled up from some kind friend.' Captain Furneaux took out his pipe and morocco pouch and, laboriously as always, set about filling the one from the other. 'I'd sent the girl home just after lunch. She wasn't well. Off colour.' (Having a period, thought Peter with certainty.) 'She didn't want to go, but I insisted. That looks good, doesn't it? I stayed on in the office on my own, doing out some adverts and stuff, but who's to know when I did them? Nobody called in, and nobody telephoned until you did, with the news. Oh, I could have done it all right without even hurrying very much, according to our clever custodians of the law.'

'But, Dad, you'd have been seen.'

'The only stage where I might have been seen, ran any real risk of it, was going from the office across the road to that end of the river path, and again coming back. And they've got something that even does away with that. You know the back of the office? Just waste ground, piles of rubbish, not a soul about. What I could have done, they say, I could have gone out the back door and on to the river path that side of the road. Then—this is the really ingenious part—I could have gone *under* the road by way of the culvert thing the river goes through, without even getting my feet wet. There's a sort of cat-walk there, apparently. Then I get on to the path again this side, and Bob's your uncle. Same thing going back.'

'But what about your arm, Dad?'

'Somebody entitled Detective-Constable Barrett, who ought to be running the show at Scotland Yard from the sound of him, has established beyond reasonable doubt that a completely one-armed man could have managed it with no great difficulty. So there we are, eh? How does it feel, having a murder suspect for a father?'

Peter was again finding it hard to think. 'They told you all that?'

'Oh yes, believe you me, every step. They're trying to scare me into doing something potty like running away. That's their little game, old boy.'

Neither spoke for a time. Captain Furneaux pressed down the tobacco in his pipe and poured himself another cup of tea with brisk, decisive movements that went with his manner while telling his story. He had sounded not frightened, or woebegone, but triumphant, like a prosecuting lawyer at the top of his form and confident of the verdict. Peter wondered if you might not feel a sort of savage satisfaction if you had the idea that life was against you and then it suddenly really seriously seemed to be. He said,

'But why would you ever have wanted to do it?'

'Ask me another. The poor devil got tight and started being offensive to half a dozen people at that dance— you remember—and I had the bad luck to be one of them.'

'Yes, what was he sort of driving at?'

'I haven't the faintest idea. I can say that anyone who went into my Service career would find I'd done nothing to be ashamed of.'

The first statement sounded like a lie, the second like the truth. Peter had neither the art nor the resolution to press the matter. Before he could think where to turn the conversation, his father abruptly went on, in a contemptuous tone,

'Actually, of course, the whole thing's a parcel of tosh. Our friends in blue have no case worth considering. You know that balderdash about motive, means and opportunity. Well. Motive: none they can ... put their finger on. Means: they found some sort of spiked club yesterday which they won't be able to trace to me because I've never even seen it. And how did a man with a game arm strike such a blow, you may ask? Oh, I could have tripped him up first, knocked him over, I'm a more powerful man than he was with the trifling exception that he had two good arms, and so on and so forth. Opportunity: yes, I could have done it, but they have no witnesses and they won't find any. It's pure unmitigated tripe. Laughable.'

In that case, why does it worry you so much? was what Peter wanted to ask, but, as before, he could not. What he did ask was only, 'Can't they see that?'

'Maybe they can and maybe they can't, it makes no odds. They've got to go through the motions of earning their screw. People are beginning to talk. Why they don't call in Scotland Yard beats me. It's that Manton fellow. Obstinate as a damn mule. And that's not the worst thing about him by a long chalk.'

Here Captain Furneaux broke off, as if remembering, after briefly forgetting, that he was talking to his son, who said,

'What happened at the inquest?'

'Oh, that. A mere formality. The whole thing was polished off in about five minutes flat. They read out your statement, and the coroner directed the jury to bring in a verdict of murder by a person or persons unknown. Which they duly did. Well ... thank you for listening, old boy. I don't mind telling you, it's eased my mind.'

'Good. You mustn't let it bother you.'

'I won't. Now you'd best be getting on with your homework. We've all got to keep going as usual. Stick to it.'

Peter did as suggested, taking his case up to his bedroom and unloading it on to his little deal bureau. It was a warm evening, the rain still holding off. As best he could, he concentrated on his French prose. He was cheered by the reflection that the case against his father did indeed sound pretty weak, and even more by the open manner, devoid of attempts to persuade or distort, in which he had heard it put. All the same, he found several obvious howlers, like *du enfant* and *elle était heureux*, on going over his rough draft. He rectified them. Then he studied the required page of *Paginae Primae* for something like the required time, and then he went down and ate supper (liver and bacon and cold apple pie) with his parents, and then he was allowed to listen for a time to Romance in Rhythm, with Geraldo and his Orchestra—not his Gaucho Tango Orchestra, just his Orchestra, and featuring Olive Groves and the Romantic Young Ladies, so that when objection to all that nigger ragtime stuff was voiced, Peter noted the phrase, to pass on to Reg, and instantly switched off. It would not do, however, to let his father get away altogether undamaged, so, after looking at the *Radio Times*, he suggested they should switch on again at 8.45, tune in to London Regional, and listen to the B.B.C. Orchestra Section G, conducted by Leslie Heward and with Heddle Nash (tenor), performing stuff called things like K.205. Captain Furneaux's reply, that it was getting late and there was school in the morning, was made in a tone that showed, as clearly as anyone could have wanted, his awareness of having quite failed to disguise his real motive for vetoing K.205 and the rest: his dislike of that kind of music as well as nigger ragtime. It was the perfect moment for asking permission to have a bath, since refusal could only look like retaliation, which could only look like acknowledgment of having taken a knock. Peter wondered now and then if everybody who lived with anybody kept carrying on in that sort of way.

His intentions towards his bath were strictly dishonourable, as for some reason they often were after a tea-time session with Reg; he would lock the door, not spin things out too long, and be prepared, should his father show a sudden desire to carry off the tooth-glass, to plead thoughtlessness, habit, sieve-like memory. The bath filled. He turned off the geyser and, in the silence, heard his mother's step on the landing, her entry into the lavatory and the turning of the key there. He got into the bath and started soaping himself. Then he heard the following, all from downstairs: a series of faint rapping sounds; his father leaving the sitting-room and approaching the front door; what could have been a struggle, with a voice or voices; a sort of prolonged crash; his father calling for help.

By this time Peter was out of the bath. He grabbed a towel and tucked it round his middle, feeling frightened, and also amazed that you could take the trouble not to be seen naked at a time of what must be emergency. Unlocking the door took a little longer still; he forgot at first that you had to pull it towards you to turn the key. From the top of the stairs he saw his father stretched out on his back with the hall-stand lying across him and blood on his face, and no sign of anybody else at all.

It was soon clear that Captain Furneaux was not seriously hurt. The blood came from a long but shallow cut, almost a scratch, beside his left ear; with only one good arm he was finding it difficult to struggle out from under the hall-stand, a solid affair with mirror and glove-box, its effective weight increased by the three or four assorted coats that had been hanging from it. He got to his feet easily enough when his family arrived and released him. He said shakily,

'I'm all right. I'm all right.'

'Who was it, Dad? Who did it?'

'I don't know.'

'Where is he? Where did he go?'

'God knows. Out the front.'

The front door—Peter took in the fact for the first time —stood shut. He made towards it, but his father caught him by his bare arm.

'You're not going out there with a damn maniac on the loose.'

'Not out, Dad. Just take a look, see if I can see him. Description.'

'All right, but stay inside, so we can slam the door in his face if we have to. Careful.'

It was later established that, from the moment when Peter (and his mother) heard the crash in the hall until the moment when he looked out of the doorway and, although daylight had hardly begun to fade, saw nobody anywhere, thirty or possibly thirty-five seconds had elapsed, quite enough for an assailant to have run the hundred-odd yards that would have taken him out of sight of that point—run them, in fact, without undue exertion. Peter shut the door. His eye fell on an object lying on the floor near the low table with the photograph and the flower-vase on it.

'It's what he hit me with,' said his father, dabbing at his face with a handkerchief. 'Let's have a look at it. You can pick it up. He was wearing gloves.'

The object was a kind of club with a nail driven through

it and some cement to hold the nail in place. Peter turned it
over curiously, his father helplessly and with a look of
horror. Seeing that look, Peter said,

'Mum, you take Dad and make him a cup of tea. I'll
phone for the police.'

Within minutes, ten or twenty, four policemen had
arrived: a sergeant and a constable in uniform, and the two
plain-clothes men, Cox and Barrett, whom Peter (and his
father) had seen before. Cox at once sent the uniformed
men out to search the area and make inquiries at neighbour-
ing houses. Then he assembled the Furneaux family in the
sitting-room. The detective-constable, Barrett, opened his
note-pad.

'I was in this room, in this very chair,' said Captain
Furneaux in due course, 'when I heard a knocking on the
front door, on the wood, though as you saw there is a
knocker. I thought that was funny, but I went and opened
the door. There was a man there who just ... leapt at me
and tripped me up and went for me with that, that thing
you've got there. I tried to hold him off, but with just my
left arm I couldn't stop him giving me this cut. Then he
pulled the hall-stand over on top of me. I was shouting out.
Then he stood and sort of looked.'

'How do you mean, sort of looked?' asked Cox. 'What
sort of looked?'

'Well, not only at me, but round the hall too, and over at
the stairs. Almost as if he was trying to remember it. Just
for a few seconds. Then ... he went. He shut the front door
after him. Quietly. I remember thinking that was funny.
And that was all. He must have dropped that spike thing; I
didn't notice. Then my son and my wife came ... It was
over in a flash.'

'Description of the man?'

'I can't tell you much, I'm afraid. It all happened so suddenly, and the light wasn't good. Oh, all right, damn it, it was lateish, but I hadn't switched on the light in the hall, out of habit—unlike many of us I have to watch the pennies, and electricity costs the earth these days. And I had no reason to expect anything out of the way. All right. He was wearing a long raincoat, and gloves, and a hat, and something round his face: I could only see his eyes really, sort of peering. He was pretty strong, muscular.'

'Anything about his height and build, colour of the eyes and hair, colour of the clothes, anything at all like that?'

'I didn't notice colours much; you don't when the light's poor. Any ex-Serviceman will tell you that. As regards height, now. He was ... he must have been an inch or two taller than me. Say five ten or eleven. And sort of wiry, quite powerful. I should say definitely young. Well, young from my point of view. Oh yes, the clothes. The raincoat was light and the hat was dark. Sorry.'

'Okay. Now did he say anything? At any stage?'

'Yes, he did. There was a certain amount of what you might call shouting at the start, during the struggle and so on. Inarticulate. But then, when he was standing looking down at me, he did say something definite. I'm not going to tell you the exact words here and now,' (Peter felt quite sad at being so easily able to guess why not) 'but it was along the lines of, "Don't you think you've got away with it, you something-or-other. You're no better than that ... than Inman. I'll get you," or words to that effect. And that was ... '

'What about the voice? Anything there?'

'Well, it was peculiar, as if he'd got a cold or something. And it struck me, I don't know how to put it quite, but like an actor when he wants to make sure everybody can hear when he's only talking quietly. That's the best I can do. What struck me was the incredible menace, the complete absolute hatred in the fellow's voice.'

'Mm.' Cox breathed in and out slowly and noisily, as if he were settling down for a short nap. His ferret–rabbit aura was as strong as ever, though he seemed perfectly clean; perhaps it all came from his prematurely gnarled hands. 'Now, madam,' he asked, 'where were you when all this happened?'

'Upstairs,' said Mrs Furneaux, in a way that would have conveyed her meaning to the blind, even perhaps the deaf.

'So perhaps you can't add very much to your husband's statement.'

'I heard the sounds, the knocking and the shouting and the crash.'

'But you didn't actually see the intruder.'

'No, I arrived on the scene too late.'

'I see. What about you, sonny Jim?'

'Same with me,' said Peter. 'I was in the bath.'

'Oh, you were, were you? That's a coincidence, isn't it? Both you and your mother out of the way at the very time this visitor pitches up? Almost to the second. Yeah.'

Barrett broke in. 'Still, never mind,'—he sounded reassuring—'we got something to go on. It's a start.'

He looked across at his superior, who picked up the spiked club from the arm of his chair. It struck Peter as curious that neither man had so far paid this surely unfamiliar and noteworthy implement more than passing attention. Cox said,

'This what-you-may-call-it here, Mr Furneaux. You've never seen it before, of course.'

'No, but I know what it is. It's a replica of the thing that was used to kill poor Inman. Or it may even be the thing itself. The chap may simply have mooched into the police station and carted it off. Easiest thing in the world, I shouldn't wonder.'

'That's not the way to go on, Furneaux, believe me. Policemen are only human when all's said and done. They're nice when other people are nice, and the opposite applies too—get what I mean? Right, you say you know what this thing is ...'

'I mean I guessed, for goodness' sake, after one of your people kindly described it to me this morning. Anyway, I'm right, am I not?'

'Now, very fortunately, I must say, you've only suffered a minor injury, haven't you?'

'Thank you, the bleeding's almost stopped now.'

'Good. So the bloke who attacked you gives you a bit of a cut and then leaves you alone when he's got you more or less at his mercy under that hall-stand. Very fortunate indeed. Bit strange too, isn't it?'

'Yes, it is. I can't explain it.'

'You knocked the weapon out of his hand, did you?'

'I think so. I'm not sure.'

'Mm.'

Cox thought for a minute, refraining, to Peter's mild surprise, from biting his nails or picking his nose. Then he asked more questions, most of them rephrasings of ones already asked and all of them seemingly unproductive. Then the uniformed police returned and stood awkwardly near the doorway of the sitting-room.

'Anything?' asked Cox.

'No, sir,' said the sergeant. 'Neighbours on that side'— he gestured towards the Trevelyans'—'heard a bump but thought nothing of it. The ones on the other side were out. Nothing along the rest of the row.'

'What about the people at Number Eleven? Were they —didn't they hear or see anything?'

Rather grudgingly, the sergeant turned over his note-book. 'No, sir.'

'Neither of them?'

'No, sir. I told you, there was nothing.'

'Thank you, Duke. Well, our friend seems to have vanished into thin air, doesn't he? Anyway, let's be on the safe side, the very safe side, and put you under police protection, Mr Furneaux. I don't know what's keeping that doctor, but he'll turn up.'

Turn up he did, to dress Captain Furneaux's wound and have the offer of a sedative declined. By that time the police had gone, though it was understood that the P.C. had only gone as far as the area round the front of the house, there to stand guard. The family, in silence for the most part, shared cocoa and biscuits at the kitchen table. Peter found he needed no reminding that there was school in the morning.

He got into bed and turned off the light by his wall-switch-plus-string-and-pulley arrangement. Even now, with the clocks turned forward for the summer, it was not quite dark outside. He could hear the noise of the river, not loud but distinct, no more than twenty-five yards from where he lay. It was awful and incredible that someone had attacked his father, good that there was a policeman within call. Perhaps there was going to be a reign of terror in the district. They were always coming up in stories, so there must be some in real life. Why—to pick out the most vivid and mysterious detail of his father's account—had the attacker looked round the hall as he stood over his victim? What in it could he have been trying to remember? He put the question aside and set about imagining Mrs Trevelyan instead. What he imagined about her was rather surprising to him at first, though very enjoyable. He turned over to imagine it better and promptly fell asleep.

IX

Another Country

At the weekend, the weather, unsettled for the previous
few weeks, took a downward turn. Wimbledon had opened
on the Friday under cloudy skies; Saturday morning, at
any rate where Peter Furneaux was, turned out cool and
damp, with outbreaks of gusty drizzle that looked like
settling down to steady rain. Twenty to one there would be
no cricket that day. Peter had a lie-in until half-past nine
or so and came downstairs to find himself alone in the
house, his mother out in good time to do the weekend
shopping, his father at the office until one p.m. It was
comforting to see the policeman on duty, a waterproof cape
over his uniform, moving slowly and with what must be
inexhaustible patience, if it were not stupefied boredom,
across the Meadow. Outside (or inside) the office might
seem a more logical place for him to be, but no doubt the
men at the top knew their job.

   Having boiled an egg, made some toast, and put milk
and sugar on a bowl of Farmer's Glory wheat flakes, he
took a loaded tray into the sitting-room, an illegal move at
this time of day but, given moderate attention to crumbs
and suchlike, safe enough in the circumstances. He read in
his father's paper that the Olympic Games were to start on
1st August and that a schoolmaster called M. R. James
had died, in his mother's that freedom of worship, assembly,
speech and the Press were guaranteed under the new Soviet
constitution. There was nothing in either about recent
doings at Riverside Villas.

How was he going to get through the day? Reg was unavailable, or rather a particular part of him was, for at weekends the lack of a father-fetching interval mean the could not produce it, even for inspection, without prohibitive risk; a similar check applied at Montrose, and indecency behind some hedge across the river lost all its allure in pouring rain. Unconsummated meetings between the two were tacitly ruled out; Peter, at any rate, felt that their friendship as such missed being close enough by a small but decisive margin. Which was just as well; start getting fond of your sparring partner and you might end up a homo.

What about that perishing Code of Dishonour? Oh no. No! Not that! The weather ruled out any kind of destinationless walk; cash in hand amounted to one and ninepence-halfpenny, just not enough for even the most frugal visit to the flicks; he could not have Daphne over here to tea, quite simply because of his father and mother, and in another sense because of Daphne too. Then, with dreadful force and inescapability, it struck him that he could all too well take her out to tea at the Honeypot in the main road; worse yet, there was literally nothing to stop him going out into the hall now, at once, forthwith, instanter, like a knife, P.D.Q., before you could say Jack Robinson, and getting her on the phone. It was like the army, or what the army sounded like. Rise and face the Prosecuting Officer. You had received your orders and you understood them— correct? Yes, sir. Was there any circumstance which prevented you from carrying out those orders? No, sir. And yet you failed to do so. Why was that? Answer me, man! Very well, I will answer for you. You were *afraid*, were you not? Ye-es, sir. (How you actually said ye-es was unclear, but it was what you said all right.) Thank you, that is all.

Sighing, Peter got up and took his tray to the kitchen. By the time he had washed up, he had got through perhaps four of the four hundred minutes that must elapse before it was too late to ask Daphne out to tea. Oh, bloody hell. Groaning now, he trudged to the telephone—picture of a young man (as his father would have put it) about to thrill to the adored voice of his lady-love. One by one, but without delay, loopholes closed on him: the exchange answered, the Hodgsons' number was free, a voice came on the line, a man's voice.

'Mr Hodgson?'

'Who is that?' The tone was sharp with impatience or nervousness.

'It's Peter Furneaux speaking, Mr Hodgson.'

'Oh, Peter.' A rather hectic cordiality at once took over. 'You want to talk to that good-for-nothing daughter of mine? Right you are, I'll go and fetch the lazy slut. Hang on, Pete.'

Another loophole closed. Peter waited. Eventually he heard, at the far end, footfalls approaching in a style that might have been used, by a very gifted actress in a play on the wireless, to suggest lassitude, unwillingness.

'Yeah?'

'This is Peter.'

'I know, my dad told me.'

'Can you come out to tea this afternoon? At the Honeypot?'

'I can't, sorry.'

'Oh. I see. Another time, perhaps.'

'No, I really can't. My cousins are coming over from Dulwich.'

This piece of what was, for Daphne, servile buttering-up led to another pause. Perhaps she could not find the energy to move the receiver into its hook. But then she surprised him further by adding, in a lowered voice,

'Is your pop all right?'

'Yes, not too bad. Thanks. For asking, I mean. He's ——'

'Because mine isn't. Talk about a bear with a sore head.'

'What's the matter?'

'These coppers, they keep on at him every day. Asking him where he was and that.'

'Where he was when?'

'Any blasted time. Then he goes and takes it out on us, see.'

Raising his eyebrows to help himself sound casual, Peter said, 'It looks as if we ought to get together and have a chat about it.'

'Does it?'

'What about meeting at the Honeypot after school on Monday?'

'Oh, I don't know.' (It was amazing, how steadily the animation was draining out of her voice.) 'I don't fancy the Honeypot somehow. Those old girls.'

'Well ... suggest somewhere else, then.'

'I'm not going to that Express Dairy. Anyway, I don't know what I'll be doing then.'

'All right, but I'll try again. And I'm sorry you've been having a hard time with your father. I do sympathize, Daphne.'

That last one got her, thought Peter, ringing off: not a bad cheek-ache effort. This, another of his father's expressions, meant making the other chap feel bad by answering a snub with a display of graciousness. His sense of triumph soon abated. Back in the sitting-room, he stared out of the french window at the saturated, scrubby little garden and tried to feel pleased, or relieved, or something, at the news that the police were bothering Daphne's father as they had been his own, but it was difficult. Dejection shouldered its way in.

He had better face the fact that *Find one* was the only bit of the Code he was ever going to be able to follow in Daphne's case, and set about finding another one. How? Just that, simply that, not a whit more than that: how? In school stories and such, your friends all had sisters. Yeah, and the stories were right up to that point, only his own friends' sisters were all fat, eight, adenoidal, going steady, too tall, silent, out whenever he called, spotty, giggly, smelly or twenty. And/or, rather: Reg's two scored five out of that lot between them. Bloody hell, it might be better to ditch the flaming Code altogether and be content with people like Reg himself. It would certainly be cheaper—to think of the hard-fiddled cash he had shelled out in the past in return for some hand-holding and a ten-second good-night embrace on a doorstep!—as well as being, in comparison, no trouble at all. A simple question that nobody ever really resented, a quick session, and then the rest of the evening or afternoon smoking, telling jokes, listening to the gramophone and playing with soldiers or trains. Or you could just go home if you felt like it. The only snag was that girls were attractive and boys were not.

While Peter was still trying to claw his way out of this mental pot-hole, the front-door knocker clattered sharply. Mrs Trevelyan, wearing her smart, dark-grey tailor-made under a light-blue mackintosh and carrying an open umbrella, was standing on the doorstep. He felt his cheeks and forehead go hot, as if he knew she knew all the things he had been thinking about her over the past week. But she showed no sign of having noticed it when she said,

'I won't come in, Peter, because I've got to get to those shops before it really starts to pour. I was just wondering, if you've nothing better to do perhaps you'd like to pop in and keep me company at tea-time. I'm all on my own today.'

'Oh ... thank you, that would be very nice.'

'About four o'clock. Do you think I should ask your mother?'

He was never able to work out whether it was her voice or her manner or some other thing that struck him, but he felt a sudden violent emptiness in his insides, as he remembered having done one morning at the station when he had put his hand into his breast pocket for his season ticket and found he had left it in his other jacket, and yet that was completely different, because what Mrs Trevelyan had done had been to make her question seem like one about tactics, not etiquette, like an admission of conspiracy. He had no better an idea of how he reacted outwardly, but the way she blinked and looked down showed that this time she had noticed something.

'No, it's all right,' he said, not very promptly. 'I'll just tell her. She won't mind.'

Mrs Trevelyan answered over her shoulder as she turned to go. 'Good. I'll see you later, then.'

He spent the next six hours in a state of almost continuous erethism (a splendid word recently unearthed by, of course, Forester, that indefatigable scourer of dictionaries). It was not altogether continuous, in that Peter quite often managed to jostle thoughts of the tea-party off stage for as much as a quarter of a minute. His mind was perpetually crossed and recrossed by doubt, disbelief, strong suspicion that he had imagined the whole thing; his body seemed perfectly certain, so much so that at lunch with his parents he had to pull his chair in so far that the edge of the table cut into his stomach, and before getting up at the end of the meal had to conjugate large stretches of *pouvoir* to himself.

Just then, a more substantial respite turned up. The telephone rang—obviously Mrs Trevelyan to cancel their date. But no: his mother, crossing the hall at the time, answered, said yes and thank you a few times each, rang off and came into the dining-room with an expression of gratified awe.

'What do you think, Peter? That was Colonel Manton. He wants you to go to his house and have tea with him tomorrow ... '

'What the devil for?' asked Captain Furneaux.

'He seems to have taken a fancy to you, Peter. He said what an intelligent boy you were. Anyway, I said I was sure you'd be delighted.'

'*You* said. It's my own view that the boy himself should have a say in the matter. He's got a mind and a will of his own, hasn't he? He's not a damn babe in arms any more.'

'But I'd love to go, Dad.'

'There you are, dear.'

'How can he love to go when he doesn't know the first thing about the chap? What piffle. I don't like the idea at all. Tea-party next door today, I'm told, tea-party up the road with a ... '

'This is quite different, dear. Colonel Manton is a very distinguished man and very well educated. It would do Peter a lot of good to come in contact with somebody like that. He told me he's very fond of young people, but he's a bachelor and so he doesn't get many chances.'

'He gets plenty of chances from all I hear.'

'What do you mean by that?'

'Oh, I don't know. It just sounds like absolute tommy-rot.'

'You're overwrought, dear, and no wonder, after that horrible experience the other night. I'm going to put you to bed this afternoon.'

'I'm perfectly all right. Perfectly all right.'

'You'll feel differently about it tomorrow; you see.'

Only by staring hard at the sticking-plaster on his father's face had Peter escaped enjoying to the very full these exchanges between his parents. First there had been that unprecedented account of his status as somebody with a mind and will of his own; he had taken complete note of that, while remaining no less completely aware that, if he should ever bring it up in the course of some future clash with his father, he would be told that anybody but a perfect nitwit would see that that was totally different. Then had come his mother's getting away with not answering his father's question—how can he love to go, etc.— by answering two or three other questions instead. (Peter had noticed other wives doing this to their husbands with just as much success and just as little effort: it must be something to do with feminine psychology.) The final to-and-fro had been best. There, his father's opposition to the projected Manton tea had fallen immediate victim to his mother's innocent snobbery, because homosexuality, even rumours of it, anything at all to do with it, could never be directly mentioned, only obscurely alluded to. Some of those allusions, along with others to masturbation, had in the past been so obscure that they might have quite frightened a boy less thoroughly versed than Peter in both subjects.

Up in his bedroom afterwards, erethism returned in full

and *pouvoir* was no bloody use at all. A simple solution
naturally came to mind, but was soon rejected: he must not
defeat his own end. As time went by, intimations of panic
flickered. He saw himself walking backwards into Mrs
Trevelyan's hall, remembered an unhelpful story about a
man with the same problem who had ended up hopping
into his young lady's presence with his inoperative leg
pointed at the ceiling, a little later was forcibly reminded
of another, no more serviceable, about a bridegroom standing on his head to pee. He washed and changed; no better;
worse if possible. Then, when zero hour was really close,
nervousness and the fear of embarrassment came to his
rescue, with such a will that, incredibly, he found himself
hoping he would rise to the occasion when and if, if, if, if,
if, if it ever arrived.

When Mrs Trevelyan opened the door of No. 21 to his
knock, she looked so pretty that he nearly ran away. She
was wearing a dress of some very non-shiny material in
what he had heard his mother call Marina blue, with a belt
of the same stuff and various pleats across the bust. Her
face was lightly made up: good taste, he thought.

'Hallo, Peter, how nice of you to come. I'm afraid the
house is in a bit of a mess—we've been doing some redecorating and we haven't finished clearing up properly. Are
you absolutely starving for your tea? Sure? Because I
thought before we settle down I could just show you what
we've been doing; I feel rather pleased with it. It won't
take a minute, so it shouldn't be too much of a ghastly bore
for you, but it's something women always insist on, showing
visitors round, as you've probably noticed. What do you
think of this, for instance?'

Peter looked round the neat, unremarkable bedroom in
which they now stood, but, in the dim light through the

drawn curtains, could see no mess, nor evidence of redecorating. 'It's very nice,' he said.

'It's not really very nice,' said Mrs Trevelyan. 'But you are.'

She took the three steps necessary to bring her across the floor to him, three steps that seemed to last indefinitely, not so much like slow motion as like no motion at all, like a row of pictures in a book showing exactly how walking worked: left foot down, right foot passing it, right foot down. When she had taken the three steps, she said in a matter-of-fact voice,

'I thought it would be silly to waste time.'

Standing at an angle from him, she put her left arm round his waist and stroked his cheek with her right hand. He made to kiss her, but she drew her head back.

'No, you're not to do anything,' she said less matter-of-factly. 'I'll do everything. And you're to let me do everything. Oh, Peter, you're so nice.'

Now she put her other arm round his waist and kissed him. He had always taken it for granted (because of the cinema) that you put your arm round the girl's waist, or top half, and she put hers round your neck, but Peter adapted himself to this other arrangement like a shot and put his arms round Mrs Trevelyan's neck. Her next move followed very soon indeed. He spent the ensuing God-knew-how-long in a state of joyful consternation. What he had imagined so often and so long, and what actually happened on Mrs Trevelyan's bed, resembled each other about as much as a fox-terrier and a rhinoceros. He had pictured the business as something rather like drifting down a river in a small boat on a summer afternoon; the reality turned out to be something equally like leading a cavalry charge across rough country under a heavy artillery barrage—or perhaps not quite equally like, because in that case the horse would naturally be underneath you. Most of this did not occur to him there and then.

Stillness and silence came, the latter particularly noticeable to Peter, who had wondered several times how thick were the walls between this house and his parents'. Mrs Trevelyan moved away from him and turned her back. Before long he realized she had started to cry. He asked her several times to tell him what was the matter, unavailingly. Asking her to turn round towards him got results in the end. Women, he had heard and read, sometimes cried for one special feminine reason or another, not out of grief or pain, and he would have been the very first to admit that he had had remarkably little experience of them, but in fourteen years he had had some experience of human beings, more than enough to show him that the wet, contorted face near his own belonged to somebody in deep and genuine distress.

'Please don't cry. Please tell me what's the matter.'

'It's so awful,' she said in a low-pitched, shaking tone, 'what I've done to you. I'm a wicked woman, evil and bad. I've taken a decent young boy and I've corrupted him. Just thinking of my own pleasure. It's absolutely unforgivable. I've seduced you. I'm a harlot and a whore, though I don't suppose you know what they are.'

Without having to think at all, Peter said, 'Oh yes I do, and you're not one, I mean you're neither. I'd have seduced you if I'd known how to do it and hadn't been much too afraid. I'd have made a muck of it. All you did was start the two of us off. And you don't think I was a sort of plaster saint, do you? I masturbate and I've done things with other boys and I've *thought* of all sorts of things, so you haven't corrupted anyone, you've really done the opposite. And you must have known I was getting terrific pleasure out of it too. And you're not wicked, you're sweet and beautiful, and you've made me see there was nothing to be afraid of.'

The tears started again, but they were of a different sort. Peter thought he recognized it. Two years before, he had fallen down during a playground game and cut his knee badly, and had managed completely not to cry until a prefect had come over and asked him if he was all right and started to bind his handkerchief round the cut. This sort of tears only needed a little time. He gave Mrs Trevelyan some friendly cuddles and discovered how nice her hair smelt. After a minute or two, she asked him in an inquisitive kind of way if he was hungry.

'My God!' He was suddenly aware of a hole inside him about the size of a man—it was as if he had missed lunch and then taken part in a seven-a-side rugger tournament. 'I'm sorry, Mrs Trevelyan, it's awfully nice in here, but I must have my tea. I mean, you did ask me to tea.'

She had started to get out of bed, but now she turned and looked down at him. He was never to forget her as she was for that short moment, sitting on her heels and grinning with tears still on her face, her fingers spread on her bare thighs. She seemed no older than he. Then she was up and into a dressing-gown. It had a pattern of big red flowers.

'You stay where you are,' she said. 'Everything's done except just making the tea. I'll go and bring it up here. It'll be cosier like that, won't it?'

Peter agreed that it would. Left alone, he decided that he felt both more comfortable and happier than ever before in his life. He could perhaps have foretold the comfort part of it, but the happiness rather surprised him at first, until he realized he had had a sort of glimpse of love, not of course an experience of it—he was not mature enough for that—

but, well, it was like an airman flying over a foreign country without actually landing there: he would know a good bit more than the chap who had stayed at home. And yet in a different sort of way it was like being in a foreign country, or rather another country. This was not foreign; he knew what everything was; the newness just made it look and feel as if it had been created five minutes before, clearly edged and eternally interesting.

Here, by the way, had Forester ever gone the whole way with a woman? Comparing how he talked about the subject with what had just happened, you would hardly think so. From here, he looked suspiciously like a case of all talk and no do. Oh boy, imagine telling him and the others about ... Peter put a severe check on that line of thought: it was puerile, and also disrespectful to Mrs Trevelyan. A quiet hint, casually dropped at the right moment, would be a different matter.

The tea arrived. It was not as elaborate as the ones provided by Reg's mother, but it was even more plentiful. Mrs Trevelyan took off her dressing-gown and got back into bed to share it, unequally, with Peter. Now and then she kissed him, not minding if he was chewing at the time. After a longer kiss than usual, she said,

'Have you had enough to eat?'

'Well, I would like another slice of that cake.'

'I was thinking of the time.'

'Oh—when's he coming back?'

'Not till late tonight. I meant how long can you stay without your parents starting to wonder.'

'Until, oh, half-past six anyway.'

'Good, it's only a quarter to five.'

'Then we've got plenty of time.'

'No we haven't, darling Peter. I haven't. We've got an

awful lot to get through. You can have some more cake in a little while. Are you ready? Yes.'

'Can I … can it be me now?'

'No, that comes later. It's still me. Different, though.'

It was indeed different, so much so that Peter had never even heard of it, but he thoroughly approved. When it was over, he had two more slices of cake and, for the first time since entering the house, felt inclined to talk.

'You like sort of being in charge, don't you? You doing everything, like you said, not the man. Or the boy.'

'Yes, I know it's rather awful of me, but I do. I don't know why. Wanting to be the dominating female in bed as well as just in the household, perhaps that's it. I haven't thought about it much.'

'How about him? I mean, does he sort of … ?'

'He wants to be the one, like most men, I suppose. Now and then I can get him to let me be it for a little while, but only as a kind of game. And it isn't a game. I always have to be careful not to let him see it isn't a game as far as I'm concerned.'

'What if he did?'

'He wouldn't like it. He'd think I was abnormal. I probably am. I don't know. It's only wanting to be the one.'

'But a boy doesn't mind, because it's all strange to him anyway, and he's so terrifically keen on everything to do with it, and he isn't like a customer in a shop who can complain or go to another one.'

'I expect so.' She looked at him carefully out of her very dark-brown eyes. 'I've been with … a couple of other boys, you know. But you're nicer than any of them. You're—please don't mind me saying it—you're the most beautiful of the lot.'

'Oh, darling Ada.' He had never thought of her by this name before, nor did he really do so now.

'You're not to call me that, Peter.'

'Sorry. You mean I don't know you well enough? What would we have to —— ?'

'No, it isn't that,' she said severely. 'You'd get into the habit and then you'd call me it one day in front of people, and then you'd blush bright pink and they'd notice and wonder.'

It sounded fairly plausible, and the bit about the blush was dead accurate, but he sensed she was not being quite truthful. Well, his not at all to reason why. He said, 'But I can't call you darling Mrs Trevelyan.'

'That's just exactly what you can call me. Go on. But say it properly.'

'*Darling* Mrs Trevelyan.'

'Oh, yes ... '

Later, they went into the bathroom and had a lovely time there, and then, later still, it was twenty-five past six and they put all their clothes on again. He carried the tea-tray down into the kitchen and put it on the draining-board. Here his glance fell on an oblong of unpainted putty round one of the panes of the central window.

'You've had the ... ' he said, and stopped.

'My husband repaired it himself; he had to buy the glass, of course. He's a terrific handyman: he did the path out there, and he put in that little cloakroom under the stairs, all but the plumbing. But I can't even mend a ... What's the matter?'

The rules of that other country were different, Peter saw. In it, someone very much concerned had just been *him*; down here, he was Mr Trevelyan, her husband, the man who shared the life of the woman he had committed adultery with, who did things round their house. 'He's always been so nice to me,' he said.

'He's nothing to do with it,' she said, taking him by the shoulders. 'Everything's all right. Nobody's been hurt. You know the old saying, what you don't know can't hurt you? Well, it's true. And you trust me, don't you? You know I'll see to it he never finds out?'

'Yes.'

'Good. You'd better go now. I don't want you to, but you'd better.'

'Can I come again?'

'Oh yes, you must. I'll arrange it and let you know ... Tell me, is your father all right after that horrible thing?'

'I think so. He's still a bit sort of shocked.'

'He must be. But at least everybody knows now he couldn't have ... it must have been someone else who did that murder.'

An idea that Peter had managed to keep buried suddenly forced itself into words. 'The trouble is, no one saw or heard the person except him.'

'What?' Mrs Trevelyan looked astonished.

'It's all just what he said happened.'

'But you and your mother must have heard him, the attacker.'

'Well, not so's we could be certain. At least, I couldn't swear to it myself; I don't know about her.'

'Peter, what are you saying?'

'He could have done it all himself. I don't really mean I think he did, just he could have.'

'But that's insane, surely. Why on earth should he? Why should he have done it himself?'

'To make people think it was an armed assault by the same man who killed Mr Inman, so whoever that man is it couldn't be him. Like you said.' He realized while he was speaking that he had worked all this out and yet not known he had until now.

'But ... ' She still looked very puzzled. 'There's a policeman outside guarding him at this very moment. What for?'

'The detectives may not have thought of what I've just said, but that's very unlikely. The inspector who came up was ... well, you could tell. Oh, there's a policeman outside all right, but that doesn't mean he's guarding my pa. He stays there when my pa isn't here. And it wasn't what you'd call a serious wound, what he got. And why should anybody want to wound him, or *wound* anybody?'

'What's he doing there, then, the policeman?'

'I don't know. Watching for something else.'

'Something else? What?'

'I don't know.'

A sharp object was pressing into his hip: a corner of the base on which the clothes-mangle was mounted. He had backed away almost to the wall of the little square kitchen while she advanced on him a couple of inches at a time. When she spoke next it was in a pleading, very serious tone.

'Peter, you must listen to me. Don't you love your father, and trust him? Don't you know him after all these years? Can't you see that a fine man like that couldn't ever, would be quite incapable of striking down another human being in that terrible way? I'm quite sure that even the police have got enough sense to see that.'

'I think I love him. Most of the time. And I trust him to do what he thinks is best for me and my ma all the time. And I think I know him, but how can I know I know him? I don't see how in this world anyone can ever say they're sure they know anyone.'

'But your own father.'

'How does that help? That only makes it worse, don't you understand? It makes it more important for me to really know him without it making it any easier to. Just because you see somebody every day and they brought you into the world doesn't mean you've got a special way of seeing into their heart, it only makes you feel worse when you find out for certain you haven't and you never will have. It makes it all absolutely ... '

By this time, both were weeping. Their arms were round each other in a fashion that would have made it hard to say which was comforter and which comforted. A minute later, when they began to kiss, it would have been no less hard to determine whether boy or woman had been the first to make the change. Peter's eyes stared through the windows and into the garden, but they saw nothing; soon they closed. Soon after that, Mrs Trevelyan said,

'It wouldn't make any difference, another few minutes, would it?'

'What? Shouldn't think so.'

'Shall we risk it?'

'Yes.'

'Yes.'

X

Questions of Atmosphere

The next day, Sunday, it rained to some purpose. The wind kept up and the temperature dropped, so much so that Captain Furneaux lighted what the other two members of his household called a Dad's fire in the sitting-room: small, neither catching nor quite going out for hours on end, and rich in smoke. Peter hardly noticed the weather; each time he did, he reproached himself for never having seen before how beautiful a bleak, gusty, sopping day could be. It must all be something to do with Mrs Trevelyan. If you had her at your back, or thereabouts, you could probably face an average Arctic blizzard complete with prowling polar bear.

Throughout the morning, through lunch-time and beyond, there kept happening to him things to do with Mrs Trevelyan that were too fast and tremendous and on top of him to be called memories. Calling them that would be like calling ginger beer nice water; compared with what was going on in his mind, ordinary remembering was like shuffling round a huge dusty room full of filing-cabinets and looking for the right card through swot's spectacles and with boxing-gloves on. When he tried to do his homework, Latin verse refused to stay Latin verse—*colle sub aprico celeberrimus ilice lucus et nonne fuerat magnificum cum Mrs Trevelyan* ... Geometry came to include *Drop a perpendicular from A to a point midway between C and Mrs Trevelyan*. And after that, *On his death in 1824, Louis XVIII was succeeded by Mrs*

Trevelyan X. Was it normal? Was he normal? There was nobody to ask, and, he realized with some indignation, no book known to him, not even *Point Counter Point*, threw the least light on the matter.

At twenty to four, it dawned on him for what felt like the first time that in a minute he was due to go and have tea with Colonel Manton. He did his hair, put on his tie, heard a car drive up, heard a knock at the front door. The wondering reverence with which his mother had told him that the colonel's chauffeur would be collecting him proved to be quite outdone by the way she went on when this actually took place. Peter had not seen her in anything like such a state since the breakfast-time at which, after some awful business the previous evening connected with the Conservative Association, she had described what it had felt like to shake hands with Mr and Mrs Anthony Eden.

Again as if for the first time, he started wondering about the imminent tea-party. Was the colonel in fact the strange man that so many people so obviously thought he was? That remained to be seen, and Peter hoped it would go on remaining. But, on the whole, he decided there was little cause for alarm. Rape could be safely ruled out as a mode of approach, except in the unlikely event of the colonel's having a Nubian or two standing by to lend a hand. There was still the risk of considerable embarrassment from a sudden direct proposal or even display. These Peter felt were very nearly as unlikely. Colonel Manton might be a strange man, but he was too cultured, too distinguished, too much a part of the upper crust to go in for orthodox strange-man tactics—if a move were to be made, it would be subtle almost to the point of undetectability. For a moment, it crossed Peter's mind that to be seduced on successive afternoons by a solicitor's wife and a retired Army officer would be a stupendous double first, a left-and-right that would make him the undisputed sexual king of Blackfriars Grammar, a legend in his own lifetime and in those of boys yet unborn, one whom Forester would be humbly grateful to be allowed to treat to a Mars Bar every break till Kingdom Come. But that was purely academic: if boys were not attractive on consideration, men were even less so on none at all.

These few reflections were interrupted often enough and long enough at a time by things to do with Mrs Trevelyan for the two lots between them to use up the whole of the car journey and the arrival at Colonel Manton's house, so thoroughly that, even if pressed with offers of dirty books etc., Peter would not have been able to say with certainty more about the chauffeur than that he was between twenty and eighty and four foot and seven foot.

In the room with the books, the colonel stood in front of the fireplace, where there burned a log fire on a scale that might have outraged Captain Furneaux.

'Ah. Ah. Good afternoon, my boy.'

'Good afternoon, sir.'

The colonel had been reading a newspaper called the *Observer*, at which he took a final glance before folding it up and putting it aside. 'I must say I don't at all care for the look of the way the situation's developing in ... ' He checked himself abruptly. 'But I don't think one should go on like that, do you? It's too easy, and I hate what's easy. Seat yourself there. What a wretched afternoon. I propose to call you Peter hereafter. May I?'

'Oh, yes, sir.'

'Master Furneaux doesn't suit you at all. It makes you sound like some disgusting old medieval priest with an enormous white beard. Now I further propose to defer tea

for a little while, unless you're positively perishing of
inanition ... Good. I want to ask you some questions relat-
ing to the recent criminal activity in these parts. You may
not be able to see the precise relation in some cases, but
it would be idle to try to cozen you into thinking I've
invited you up here for a snug little chat. It won't take an
eternity, and then afterwards we can settle down and have
some fun.'

Fun? thought Peter. Fun?

'The first part is very obvious and tiresome, I'm afraid,
but inescapable. For a reason I'll go into later, I wasn't in
the neighbourhood last Thursday evening, or else I would
certainly have accompanied the police officers who came
to your house as a result of the attack on your father. As
it is, I must ask you to repeat to me your version of that
incident. Everything you can remember, however glaringly
irrelevant it may be. And as slowly as you like.'

'There's one thing I must know before I say a single
word, sir. I should have thought of it on Thursday night,
but I was too flustered then. It's this: to what degree do
you suspect my father of being mixed up in all this?
Because I'm not going to help to incriminate him. It may
be my duty to, but I want to hear you tell me it is before
I consider going any further.'

'Well urged, Peter. Let me assure you unequivocally
that, for more than one reason, we're quite certain that
your father had no hand in the death of the late Inman.
Does that satisfy you?'

That voice of the colonel's was, to Peter, not well suited
to assuring people unequivocally of things. Because it
never changed, except to intensify what it had been all
along, it was an ideal voice for lying. That, among other
things, made it very unlike his own father's voice. Perhaps

the difference helped to account for the fact that, of the two men, one lived alone and the other did not. 'Not quite, sir. A friend of mine told me one of your men was saying you all thought my father was mixed up in it. In those very words.'

'You need pay no attention to that man, whoever he may be. We had to explore the possibility that your father was involved in the murder. We did so, and have established that he was not. Consider this. Do you suppose I could have it said that I tricked a fourteen-year-old boy into supplying evidence against his father on a charge of this sort? On any charge?'

'I see that, sir; it's a good argument. Here goes, then.'

While he told his story, Peter avoided looking at the colonel, whose eyes stayed fixed on him, and looked round the room instead. The rooms he was accustomed to had in them two kinds of object, ones you used, like chairs, and ones you looked at, like his mother's china cats. Here, there was a third kind: an old book in a glass case all to itself, a barometer that would not have been out of place on the bridge of a light cruiser, a solitary foot-high soldier—nineteenth-century Continental was as near as Peter could get—made out of some shiny stuff; that last one might possibly be there for you to look at but you would not get much out of doing so. Also noticeable was a framed photograph of a black man in evening dress with an inscription about best wishes to the Colonel from the Hawk.

Peter came to the end of his tale. Colonel Manton took a large log out of a wicker basket on the hearth, dropped it consideringly on the fire and said,

'How easy would it be to upset that hall-stand?'

'Not very. It's got a sort of gutter thing at the bottom

for umbrellas to drip into that gives it a low centre of gravity.'

'But, for instance, you could upset it.'

'Yes, sir. It might take me a few seconds.'

'You've been admirably explicit about what you saw and heard and didn't see and hear. Did you smell anything? When you came down into the hall after the attack.'

Peter considered. 'No, sir, nothing. That is, I didn't notice anything.'

The colonel went through his cigarette-lighting drill in silence. 'Now I want to ask you some more general questions,' he eventually said. 'We detective johnnies like to get the feel of the atmosphere surrounding an affair such as this. I say, that's a vile phrase when you come to think of it. Also one that I would seriously wager the late Queen Victoria would not have understood. Anyhow ... without raising the stylistic level, I might add by way of amplification that we like to comprehend the emotional background of a case. At least I do. Married couples. In the nature of things, and for the matter of that under English law, you can't yourself have been married. But you are that ideal combination, an uninformed observer who is also shrewd. Some poetic johnny was going on the other day about how much he didn't care for learned observers. Let's take the Hodgsons first. Would you say they got on well together and as far as you can tell?'

'Mr Hodgson has always been very decent to me whenever ——'

'But he's not your father, and anyway you have an obligation to further the course of justice, and you also want to. Don't you?'

'Yes, sir. I should say they get on pretty well. Mr Hodgson's sort of not as much of a gentleman as his wife's a lady, or as much as she'd like to be. I think she thinks he's vulgar and he thinks she's stuck-up, a bit. But that seems to be true of a lot of married couples I know—I'm not including my own parents. I reckon the Hodgsons are ... really pretty fond of each other.'

While Peter talked, the colonel had moved to a picture near the door. It showed a heap of foodstuffs thrown together in what must have been a sullen or jeering spirit. With his back almost fully turned, he said now,

'Without being what you might call devoted.'

'They still might be, in spite of what I've said. I don't know enough about marriage to say.'

'Ah-ha. Mr and Mrs Trevelyan. What about them, eh?'

Peter had seen it coming all right, but that was no help. His face felt as if a large gas-fire had been lighted and turned up full about eight inches from it, and his head and neck moved about of their own accord. Anybody catching sight of him across a cricket-ground would have known at once what he had been up to, in outline if not in full detail. It was a bit of luck that the colonel was not looking at him. With another bit of luck he would stay like that until the worst of the blush was over.

'They get on very well as far as I can see.' It was true if you left out the implications of yesterday afternoon, and he managed to get it said in a not too uneven voice. 'They don't give the impression of having rows or anything, and living next door to them I'd probably know if they did. They go out a lot and always go together, at least when I've happened to notice.'

Colonel Manton had still not turned round. 'The deceased Inman didn't seem to take that rather rosy view.'

'No, he didn't, sir. Not seem to. I've thought a bit about that since. And in retrospect I think he was just trying to be nasty without necessarily having anything to go on. Like wipe that grin off your face and who do you think you are.'

'It's possible. Now the Langdons.'

'They get on well too, but in a different ... But Mr Langdon can't have anything to do with it, sir, any more than Mr Trevelyan. They say one was with his wife when the murder was done, and the other had a customer with him, a client. And Mr Langdon wasn't even threatened at the dance.'

'That may have been ... ' The colonel checked himself in his turn. 'Those threats,' he said, crossing to the bell and pushing it several times. 'One after the other. Like a ritual. Almost like a man going round saying goodbye before setting off on a long journey. And it was that, in a way. I told you when we began that you might not be able to see where some of my questions were going to lead, and we're on one of those now. Back to the Langdons, Peter, if you please.'

'Yes, sir. I was going to say they get on in a rather different way from the Trevelyans. They're more like ... well, I don't mean Mr Langdon's babyish or childish or anything, but Mrs Langdon does seem to sort of mother him, and I get the impression he rather likes it.'

'Ah. Now that does set the mind to work.' The colonel gave a stare that made it quite possible to believe he meant what he said. 'Do you happen to know if Mrs Langdon has money of her own?'

'I've never heard that, sir, and it strikes me as pretty incredible. Anyone with any money to speak of wouldn't be living in Riverside Villas.'

'Now we can't have that kind of talk from you, young man,' said Colonel Manton, seemingly through a throatful

of iron filings. 'You're thinking like a cynic, and you have to
earn the right to do that. It's quite easy to earn, but it
does take time; in fact, time is all it takes.'

There were sounds outside as of a severely handicapped
person's attempts to open the door. The colonel made no
move to intervene, nor did he do anything at all when the
servant Peter he had run into on his previous visit finally
effected entry bearing the biggest and most heavily laden
tray he had ever seen and went on to unload it on to what
his mother would have called an occasional table.
Neverthless, the colonel did talk. He said,

'Interesting name, Langdon. Like some others. Have
you come across it before, Peter?'

'Yes, sir. But not as the name of a man.'

'Go on.'

'It's the name of a country in *Gulliver's Travels* by
Jonathan Swift. Mr—my English master says it was
meant to be England. It's an anagram of it except for one
letter.'

'Which, to those who know their Swift, makes it easy to
remember ... To remember. Yes, that's the shop done
with for now. Unfortunately I can't make it a rule never
to discuss business at meals, like—like some people, but
I avoid it as far as possible. I don't think *Gulliver* is a very
sensible book, do you? I always wonder how different it
might have turned out if Swift had been a farmer or a stable-
keeper instead of a parson. But there it is. Now just you
fall to, dear boy.'

There was everything on the table bar roast turkey and
Christmas pudding: sausages and baked beans, cold ham
and sweet pickle, hot buttered toast, crumpets, egg-and-
cress sandwiches, Marmite-and-tomato sandwiches, banana
sandwiches, white bread and butter, brown bread and

butter, malt loaf, different sorts of cake, different sorts of cakes, jams, jellies, jelly, blancmange, fruit salad, what turned out to be very posh fish-paste in a little flat china bowl, and half a gallon of tea. It made what Reg's mother provided look like a school dinner, or alternatively it was like Mrs Trevelyan turned into food.

Colonel Manton said, 'I quite realize you may not be able to dispose of everything absolutely down to the last crumb, but you're not to mind that. I mention it because I'm an only child like you, and my mother spent most of her time giving me frightful drubbings for not getting through a side of beef at every meal. Rest assured someone will eat what you don't. If there is anything you wish for which you do not see, kindly ask for it. We cannot hope to display our large stock in its entirety.'

The last two sentences were delivered in unexpectedly efficient cut-glass cockney. Peter made deprecating motions and started on the sausages. The colonel, eating sandwiches, watched him with a benign air, though you would not have had to change it much for it to suit a poisoner who was very full of himself.

'I expect you're as keen as mustard on young women, aren't you, Peter? Girls? That kind of person?'

This must be it, thought Peter. Trying not to sound too emphatic, he said, 'Yes, sir—very keen indeed.'

'Good for you. Or good on you, as the men in my old regiment mostly had it. Essential, too,'—the iron filings were there again by the tablespoonful—'because we must keep the human race going. Mustn't we? A strange obligation, I've always thought, but it does seem to be very widely subscribed to. Enough of that. No doubt you're keen on music too. As well as young women, I mean.'

'Oh yes, sir. How did you know?'

'Everybody is these days, as you must have noticed. What sort do you like?'

The colonel sounded as if he really wanted to hear, which was unexpected behaviour in a grown-up. It was characteristic of them (unless they were schoolmasters) to ask you what you felt or thought about something as nothing whatsoever more than an announcement that they were going to start very soon on what they felt or thought; why was it that boys never did that, and when did you change? Never mind for now.

'Well, several sorts, really. The South American stuff,' —Peter did not care to name Troise, Geraldo, Eugene Pini, Mantovani, because that might look insufficiently genteel to the colonel, like showing you knew too much about plumbing—'and some of the classical favourites, and the bands on the wireless'—plumbing argument again.

'Bands. You don't mean the Band of the Grenadier Guards or Foden's Motor Works Band.'

'No, sir.'

'You mean dance bands.'

'Yes, sir.'

'Yes. Yes. Which do you think is the best?'

Chewing a crumpet saturated with hot melted butter, Peter deliberated. 'Ambrose and his Orchestra.'

'Are you sure?'

'Yes, sir. That I think so, I mean.'

'I'm delighted to hear you say that. Imaginative arrangements, impeccable ensemble playing, and frightfully good individual work from Max Goldberg and Danny Polo, to name only a couple. Sadly underrated fellow, Goldberg. Polo's a Yankee, of course, which gives him an advantage straight away; curious how it always does. It's a pity he's not a nigger. Yes, there's no getting away from it, the

niggers play the best jazz music. I popped over to Paris to
hear a gang of them just at the end of last year. There was
the most dazzling trumpeter called Bill Coleman, and a
pianist by the name of Garnet Clark, who struck me as off
his head, but he could tinkle the ivories all right. Some of
the Frogs weren't half bad, too. There was a sort of gipsy
chap called ... But I mustn't bore you by going on about
people you've never heard of. Let's have a record.'

This last evoked Reg so sharply that, in one way, Peter
would not have been surprised to see Colonel Manton pull
out a packet of Turban, if nothing more. In every other
way, though, he would have been flabbergasted at best,
and in the event all that happened was that the colonel
went to his radiogram and put on a record, first announcing
that among those taking part was Fats Waller, whose work
Peter must surely be familiar with. Peter was, and said
so, but the piano solo that began the number sounded
nothing like the Fats Waller he knew. Coming in at the same
time as one or two other instruments, a man sang in a high
voice,

'Something was moaning in the corner—I tried my best
to see,'

then, as if by no means satisfied with his first attempt,
sang it again, ending that part with what sounded like,

'It was the mother bed-bug praying to the good Lord
for some more to eat.'

What followed departed a little further from reason,
though it was reassurance of a kind to hear someone who
must have been Waller shouting vaguely but cordially in
the background. A tenor sax with a bad cold and more

singing led to a peevish, acid trumpet that rounded off the disc.

'I see you're not impressed.'

'Not very, sir, no, I'm sorry.'

'Don't let the form put you off. It's a simple twelve-bar blues. Like ... '

Now the colonel went to his piano and threw back the lid over the keyboard with a smart crack. Sitting down on a highly polished stool of darkish wood, he began to play in an amazingly proper style, like part of a shit-hot record or at least the man in the B.B.C. Dance Orchestra letting himself go. It was so good that the danger of his starting to sing lost much of its gripe. (Why was ordinary people singing so frightening just as an idea when people in the business singing was so all right?) Hum Colonel Manton did, but at low volume, absolutely as if to himself. The number—you really could call it a number—finished with a sort of inconclusive multiple trill that was like the way the best tangos ended but was not the same. He got up and shut the lid.

'Or something to that effect,' he said.

'I say, that was super, sir. Where did you learn?'

'Here. By trying to copy what I heard on that machine.'

'Do you ever play in a band?'

'My dear Peter, can you imagine *me*' (surely it must hurt him to talk like that) '*playing in a band?*'

'I'm sorry, sir, I spoke without thinking.'

'See that you avoid the practice in future. Your plate's empty.'

'I think I'm full up, sir.'

'Nonsense. No boy of your age is ever full up. Try the fruit cake. Let's have the darkies again. You've heard of Louis Armstrong?'

'Oh yes, sir, and heard him play and sing.'

'In his vaudeville style for the most part, if not entirely. This is different. *Dallas Blues*, the reference being to the town of that name, which, as you will infer from the second vocal chorus, is in the state of Texas and is served by the Santa Fe railroad. This is quite a big band: ten of them, all as black as the ace of spades, of course. You'll notice it's in the same twelve-bar form.'

Peter could honestly have said he did, and quite enjoyed the record, though for him it had a rather old-fashioned sound to it. But Colonel Manton stood completely still, halted in the act of fitting a cigarette into his holder. When the music had finished, he said, without rasping,

'Imagine what it must feel like to be able to do that. Any of it.'

'It was good,' said Peter, finishing his slice of cake.

'Indeed it was.' The voice was back to normal, the cigarette lighted. 'More tea, young man?'

'No thank you, sir. I really am absolutely full.'

'You know, that noise is about a quarter of my life. It makes me do absurd things. For instance, the reason why I wasn't here on Thursday evening, which I'm sure you've been all agog to learn, is that I was in London, at the Holborn Restaurant, listening to Bram Martin's band, simply on the score of a recommendation by our friend Leonard G. Feather in the *Radio Times*. I could have saved my time and money and heard quite enough of them on the wireless. But then ... one gets tired of simply listening by oneself every evening.

'Now, the meal being over, a little more shop if I may. I still don't know enough about Inman, deceased. Have you ever heard anyone say that he, Inman, was, one, a woman-chaser, two, a great reader or an intellectual in any sense, or, three, a gambler?'

'No, sir, none of the three, but then I've never heard much about him, except that nobody seems to have liked him much.'

'Maddening. Next. If we agreed to divide people into even-tempered and quick-tempered, in which category would you put Hodgson?'

Peter thought about it. 'Quick-tempered, sir.'

'Ah-ha. Of those we've mentioned, who is the keenest gardener?'

'Mr Langdon, sir. Mr Hodgson does a bit, too.'

'Does—do you know or know of anybody round the place reputed to have a knowledge of poisons?'

'Poisons? No, sir. I suppose the chemists would ——'

'Quite so. Well, that's about as much as I've got for the moment.'

'Colonel Manton, would you mind if I asked you some questions?'

'In principle, certainly not, though I can't guarantee to answer all or even any of them.'

'I understand that, sir. Well ... do you know who the murderer is?'

'Oh yes—that was obvious the moment I knew the bare facts. It's a question of proof, as it inevitably is when there are no material witnesses, when the murderer doesn't at once give himself up and confess, doesn't equally avow his guilt by committing suicide, et cetera. But assembling proof isn't so difficult when one knows exactly where to look.'

'I see. What had my father done so Mr Inman could threaten him?'

'No answer, Peter, I'm afraid. Your father must tell you

in his own good time. But you can rest assured that it's nothing disgraceful and that it has no bearing on this inquiry.'

'Do you think he was really attacked, or he did it himself to divert suspicion of the murder?'

The colonel's smooth but abundant eyebrows went up for a moment. 'Let me put it to you like this: that's a matter in which the police no longer take any interest.'

'Sir, when will it all be over?'

'In a few days. With luck. And possibly with your further assistance.'

'But what could I ——?'

'It's a remote possibility. Now, having work to do, I'm going to throw you out, or rather have you driven home. But let me lend you a book'—the colonel crossed to his shelves—'that may help to keep your mind off unpleasant realities. Ah yes.'

The volume, still in its paper cover, changed hands. It was *Be Absolute for Death: an Otho Lambe mystery* by Regina Thynne.

'Thank you very much, sir; I'll take great care of it.'

'You'll find the blurb, the summary inside the jacket, is rather misleading as regards one crucial point. But I think that's more or less legitimate, don't you? After all, the whole raison d'être of a murder story is to trick the reader. Isn't it?

'Oh, and just as a matter of interest, everything I've said to you this afternoon has had a purpose—admittedly not a really pulverizingly serious one in the case of the man Armstrong and his colleagues—and everything I've told you is true. For what it's worth. Anyway, bear it in mind, eh?'

'Yes, sir.'

'Good.' The colonel worked his bell-push. 'Thank you for coming, Peter.'

'Oh no, sir, thank *you* for a sawney tea. And the music.'

'Perhaps you'll come again one of these days.'

'I'd love to. Next time I'll bring some of my own records.'

Something flickered in Colonel Manton's face, as if he had just remembered a matter best forgotten. Then it was gone, and he smiled with what could quite easily have been genuine warmth. 'What a splendid idea. I shall look forward to it. Do give your parents my ——'

The telephone, standing on a tall bamboo table, rang briefly. As he crossed to it, the colonel gave a different sort of smile and a wave that between them meant that he expected to be left alone while he took the call — naturally. So Peter too smiled and waved and went out into the hall, pulling the door shut behind him. But there was nobody about in the hall for the moment, and he found he had not really shut the door after all, and the colonel's voice was as penetrating as ever. Fortunately for Peter's self-esteem, there was no need for him to move an inch towards the doorway in order to hear what was being said on its further side.

' ... Oh dear. Well, that's rather up to you, Cox. Use your own judgment. My personal judgment is that the further away you go, the less likely Inman would have heard about it. And don't forget he could just have remembered him from the original —— No no, I'm not changing my mind, I'm merely following your assumption. No, simply because he's the one candidate who can't possibly have been Evans. No, nothing at all: he's had no more luck with the pubs than you have with the schools. I myself don't think they'd have risked a pub. But I have just learnt something that supports my own assumption quite strikingly. No, not until ... '

That was as much as Peter heard, because at that point the chauffeur, buttoning up his jacket, came out into the hall and bore him away. He took in almost as little about the man on the return journey as on the outward; his mind and emotions were too hard at work, not with the one-sided conversation he had overheard—he could make no sense of that and did not now try to—but with the conclusion he found he had come to from some of the questions Colonel Manton had asked him. It indicated a certain person as the murderer beyond possibility of mistake, and Peter, thinking of that person, was full of sorrow.

XI

Fresh Evidence

'You'll never prove it, sir,' said Barrett to the colonel forty-eight hours later. 'No motive, no weapon and a partial alibi.'

'I know the motive and I can throw doubt on the partial alibi.'

'You've deduced the motive to your satisfaction, and the doubt you ——'

'What about your satisfaction?'

'My satisfaction's neither here nor there, sir, is it? I grant you your motive's the only one we've come up with that's the right size, but we've got to find some more pointers to it, and I've covered an awful lot of ground without. No unmistakable signs of the situation that would give the motive—no witnesses to it. And I was going to say, the doubt you could throw on the partial alibi still leaves a more than reasonable doubt on the other side, so's no jury would dream of convicting. And you won't get a flaming word out of him. And no weapon. And those false weapons are no help at all.'

'We may yet get several words out of him if we play our hand cleverly,' said Colonel Manton, squinting at the polished toe-cap of his shoe. 'He may already know what we've deduced, which would make him vulnerable: not necessarily within the remotest distance of cracking, but the more inclined to make some ... useful response. Whatever happens, he's in danger of losing everything he's got, especially given his circumstances. And production of the weapon is not indispensable to the securing of a verdict of guilty. In the case of John Dickman before the War, two weapons were used, and the police never found either of them, but he was convicted and hanged just the same. All right, there may have been some other peculiar features about that trial, but there have been other verdicts of guilty in the absence of a weapon—Thomas Allaway in '22, and ... And *really*, Barrett, this morning you were saying you agreed with me.'

'I do agree with you, sir, for what that's worth, which is sweet f.a.—sorry, sir. And you could only have the slightest chance of managing without a weapon if it's either quite plain how it was done or you can show exactly and indisputably how it was done. And you can't do that. And this playing our hand. I don't like the sound of your next move at all. I only hope you know what you're doing.'

'Barrett, have you ever noticed that sometimes you sound exactly like Cox? And speaking of Cox, where is Cox? Apart from being at the top of my smacking-list.'

'He'll be on his way, sir.'

'So he will. Let's fortify ourselves against his arrival. What do you want to drink?'

'Could I have a little whisky, sir?'

'By all means, on the understanding that you cease to refer to the stuff as if it were ether.'

The colonel went to a large silver tray crowded with bottles and drinking implements. Although the air was less chill than recently, a log fire again burned in the grate. Now and then a gust of wind shook the flames or rattled the windows. Barrett tried to think about his fortnight's holiday at Bognor, due to start in a month's time.

'There. Drink it up and have another. You're going to need it.'

Barrett took the chased silver beaker and swallowed largely. 'Has it got to be me, sir?'

'You know very well it has. It can't be me and it mustn't be Cox. Help yourself to a cigarette.'

'Thank you, sir. Can I have another look at the note?'

The note, handed over by the colonel, consisted of a plain sheet of paper on which letters crudely cut from newspapers had been messily gummed. It read,

> if YOU *want* to know the TRUTH *about* the InMAn *CASE*, find out *why* LANgdOn stopPed be*ing* A school t*ee*CheR AND what ho*dg*SON *was* DOing on the *EVENING* of feBu*ary* 14th
>
> FRIEND of *justice*

The envelope was addressed to Colonel Manton in the same style and had been posted locally in time for the 8 p.m. collection the previous day.

'Any new thoughts, Barrett?'

'Well ... nothing on whether it's an untidy person or a tidy person pretending to be untidy. Not much help whichever it is. But it must be literate pretending to be illiterate.'

'Because it would have been less trouble to find February entire and use that. Yes yes. Get on.'

'And because nobody outside a kids' comic spells teacher that way, providing he can spell at all.'

'Perhaps not,' said the colonel grudgingly. 'In the sphere of kids' comics I bow to your authority. But that's not much help either. Is it?'

'No, sir. Myself, I'm not satisfied it can't be somebody nothing to do with the case.'

This drew a malevolent stare, as if some canon of morality had been flouted. 'Because, Barrett, the reason why Langdon stopped being a schoolteacher is not common knowledge. Patient research is needed, as we have learnt.'

'Well, I'm the one that's learnt it really, sir, aren't I?'

'None of that, my man, or you'll find yourself on more fatigues. Further, we had reason to look and some idea of where.'

'All it need have taken was someone who remembered like you did, was right nasty and had the free time. And maybe the professional interest, like.'

'Make a note to check the library. You're simply creating more work for yourself. Anything else?'

'We must try the paper and envelope.'

'And find only one firm in England makes them, and the only lot they've sold since the war was bought across the counter from a chap with a photographic memory. In the same way as there are all those beautiful sets of all ten fingerprints all over both sides of the paper and on the inside and outside of the envelope. You can check where the stuff came from after you've been to the library. Not a Herculean task, Barrett. There's an even chance you'll go to Smith's first and it'll turn out to be Woolworth's, but that must simply be faced. Have some more whisky, and that's an order.'

While the colonel was busy at the drinks tray, and Barrett was wishing he could tell him to ask Scotland Yard for help before somebody made him, a car drove up outside. In due course, Cox was shown in. He looked tired and resentful, both states he was well suited physically to express. A drink was in his hand, and he drank some of it, before he spoke. When he did, all he said at first was,

'Clear.'

The colonel pushed his head forward like a cat on the watch. 'Interesting.'

'Oh, ruddy fascinating. He spent a couple of hours not being able to remember. Of course, being those months back, I couldn't hardly blame him.'

But I bet you did your level best, thought Barrett.

'Indeed.'

'Yeah, indeed. He was pretty sure he'd have been in the Dog and Partridge, being a Friday, and he gives me something like eighty names of blokes who might have been there too. But the way I look at it, if he can't remember why should any of them? Still, I was just going to clear off and start on my list when it strikes him—it had been somebody's birthday. Whose? Another couple of hours on that. Then it all comes back to him. Old Bill Page. The pair of them and one or two others got tight as drums in the Dog and took a bottle of Scotch back to his place, that's Hodgson's place, and when they'd gone he went up to bed and fell over a chair undressing and woke up his missus and she didn't half crack on at him and he didn't half crack on at her and what with the both of them they woke up the daughter. So after that it was easy. Well, I say easy, it was easy enough hanging around for another couple of hours waiting for Bill Page to come home from work. When he did, he confirmed the whole boiling. So did Mrs Hodgson and the girl.'

'How did they remember the date?'

'Kid been away from school with a sore throat or something.'

'Do sit down, Cox; I can see you've had an exhausting time.'

'I'll stand, thanks. I've done enough sitting today to last me halfway to my pension.'

'Well, now ... ' The colonel topped up his own drink. 'He couldn't have picked a better evening, could he?'

'Picked?' said Cox. It was barely a question.

'On the assumption that he sent the note.'

Barrett said, 'You want to blackguard somebody, Inspector, so you make it look like you're blackguarding yourself at the same time, only it turns out you aren't, but it still looks like you're trying to, only you got the date wrong or something.'

'I don't know what they teach you boys at that college.' Cox banged the end of a cigarette against a matchbox. 'Nothing's ever straight as far as you're concerned, is it? All a great mass of ——'

'You must admit, Cox, it does make Langdon the less likely of the two.'

'Two? What two?'

'He was vulnerable and Hodgson evidently wasn't.'

'Double bluff, sir?' asked Barrett, purely in the hope of irritating Cox.

'What's all this about the two and double bluffs? If you ever get so's you're dry behind the ears, son, you may just possibly realize that in criminal investigation what you hardly ever get is a bluff, unless it's like a bloke with an empty gun going on as if it's loaded, and what you never ever get is a double bluff. Because why? Because it's too perishing risky, that's why. If you stab a fellow and walk out into the street with the knife in your hand, people aren't going to say, oh, he can't have been up to anything, no one could be such a mutt, showing themselves like that in broad daylight. Not them; they're going to say, there's a bugger with a bloodstained knife in his hand—grab him quick. Right?'

'*Right*, Cox. What is your view?'

'My view? Of this note? Chuck it away is my view. Some idle old woman, and there's plenty of them around these parts'—Cox's glance moved to the ceiling for a moment—'someone who ought by rights to be in the loony-bin digs up a bit of dirt and tries to make trouble. Just that and no more. It doesn't affect my theory. How could it?'

'The evidence for your theory is mainly negative.'

'Like for other people's, Colonel. Mine's coming along nicely, with that school yesterday.'

'We'll discuss it later. Tomorrow I want you and Barrett to check all movements between five-thirty yesterday—the late-afternoon postal collection—and eight o'clock. Everybody, including Mrs Inman. This time you might even find something.'

'No knowing, is there?'

'You'd better be off, Barrett, unless you need another bracer. I leave it to you to see to it there's as little avoidable fuss as possible.'

'I'll do what I can, sir.'

'Make sure this gets to the press, would you? and report back here when you've finished.'

'Right, sir.'

Barrett exchanged nods with Cox, who was now looking disapproving as well as tired and resentful. On his way out to the car, he glanced at the piece of paper the colonel had given him when he left. In a plain, upright hand, it said that police investigating the Inman murder had received an anonymous letter making allegations about two witnesses in the case. These, however, had proved unfounded, and the letter was being treated as the work of a crank or mentally unbalanced person. It sounded right, and might well have the effect its author intended, but to Barrett, by this time in motion with the police driver at his side, the letter itself still had its mysterious aspects. To try to implicate two people was less convincing, twenty times less, than to try it with one. Or was it intended to imply collusion, collaboration? That certainly did make the thing sound like the work of a ... Did it? A pair of assailants, one to hold down the victim, the other to strike that fearful blow, was in itself a plausible idea, one that could throw light in other directions. But it assumed that the colonel was wrong.

The car pulled up outside the police station before Barrett had concluded anything more than that he had reached a state of near-total uncertainty. In the gloomy, dingy hall of the building, hung with photographs of dead or otherwise departed guardians of the law, he was immediately confronted with one of the journalists he had learnt to dislike the look of in the seven days since the murder—the oldish one who kept sniffing, Grundy by name. Still, his presence here and now was convenient enough.

'Anything for me?'

'Yes. This.'

Frowning, the man gazed at the paper, taking a good deal longer over the four lines of clear manuscript than might have been expected from one supposed to be able to write as well as read.

'Not much there, is there, old boy?'

'Something.'

Just then, Inspector Knightley, adjusting his uniform cap, came out of his office across the hall. He signed to Barrett, called to P.C. Hawkins, who stood nearby conversing with the duty sergeant, and approached. Grundy sniffed and looked again at the colonel's statement.

'Not much, old boy. What I want to know is, when are you expecting to make an arrest?'

Barrett hesitated, but the inspector came up just in

time to hear the question. With a glance at Barrett so blank as to look more than half demented, he announced,

'Within a brief period of time, sir. Very brief indeed.'

'Eh? When's that?'

'We're about to set off for the purpose at this moment.'

'Where to? Can I follow you? My car's outside.'

'Then you look like bringing off a *scoop*, old boy,' said Barrett in an approximation to the colonel's manner. But he did not feel light-hearted or amiable or even satiric.

Soon afterwards, he was sitting in the back of the police car next to Hawkins, with the inspector beside the driver and Grundy on their track in his horrible Ford. They plunged under the railway bridge, climbed, turned off, and at once trees and bushes and strips of unmown grass could be seen. You were never far from the country in England, thought Barrett. Another turn-off and a short descent brought more greenery into view, and, from the look of them, Riverside Villas could have been miles from any other habitation.

Here the party met with a check. Grundy, previously warned to keep his distance, approached the inspector as, with Hawkins and Barrett, he returned to the police car.

'What's up, then?'

'Not at home. Gone to the tennis club, the neighbour says.'

'That means you'll ——'

'Let's wait here, sir,' said Barrett. 'They won't be able to go on playing much longer.'

'It might be ten o'clock or later. I'm not cooling my heels until then in a spot like this, and it's my duty to get the job done as soon as possible. Let's be off.'

'It'll be so public there, sir.'

'I can't help that, can I, Barrett?' said the inspector with another frenziedly blank look.

The two cars retraced their course for some minutes before striking off at a right angle. It was near-country here too, with lengths of hedgerow between the houses. Beyond a derelict mill the cars drew up. Leaving the police driver behind his wheel, the other four walked between a pair of open wooden gates, down a short cinder path and into the tennis-club grounds. These lay in a slight depression and so were sheltered from the wind, which by this time had largely subsided. Now and then the sun showed between lumps of thick cloud. On two sides lay parts of the local golf-course, upon which, near an immense oak tree, a group of figures moved. Beyond them, the grassy slopes rose to a line of woods on the skyline. All five tennis-courts were in use, and perhaps forty people, in deck-chairs or in chatting groups, were watching the play. Barrett recognized several of them: a tobacconist and his wife, a doctor, the vicar of St Stephen's, a couple of insurance clerks sometimes on hand for a pint or two in the saloon of the Dog and Partridge, Mr and Mrs Trevelyan, Mr and Mrs Langdon, the last four dressed for tennis. In his state of uncomfortable preoccupation, the scene made little impression on Barrett at the time, but in the future he was often to recall vividly its blend of the animated and the tranquil.

'Three police officers of the standards of fitness required by the Force,' he said, breaking a silence. 'Should be enough to overcome any resistance.' He realized he had spoken with some bitterness.

'Oh, I don't reckon on any of that,' said Knightley.

'Can I go on ahead, sir? So we needn't ——'

'There's no reason to depart from laid-down procedure.' Grundy drew level. 'Who are you after, Inspector?'

'That will shortly become quite clear.' Knightley was at his most ponderous. 'And kindly remain in the background. You're here on sufferance, remember.'

Heads were turning towards them and voices raised, then lowered. A movement in the nearer distance attracted Barrett's eye: some youngsters playing catch or french cricket on the patch of rough grass beyond the furthest court. He felt sure he recognized the Furneaux boy's fair head.

The inspector, in the lead, had reached the long, single-storey wooden shack that was the pavilion. Behind the rail of the central part of this, seven or eight people stood or sat, all staring at him. He mounted the couple of steps between ground and floor, approached one of those standing there and, into an almost total silence, said,

'Walter David Furneaux, I arrest you for the murder of Christopher Inman. I must caution you that anything you say may be taken down in writing and used in evidence, but you are not obliged to say anything at the moment. Come along, sir, please.'

There was nothing like silence now. Crying out, Mrs Furneaux clung to her husband, who was silent and without expression; everybody else had something to say. Barrett had his notebook ready, but there was nothing to be taken down in writing by him; Grundy, however, scribbled away at top speed. Knightley tried as gently as possible to detach his prisoner; Hawkins did his best to hold back and quieten a score of vocally excited and astonished men and women. So it went for twenty seconds, longer. Then, in no time at all, the inspector was leading his man away with Hawkins on the other side. Barrett found himself face to face with the younger Furneaux.

'Why have you arrested my father? He hasn't done

anything.' The tone of this matched the mildness of the words, but the boy's face was full of accusation and outrage.

'Look, youngster'—Barrett was aware of Grundy almost at his side—'Colonel Manton asked me to tell you something if I saw you. It's this: you're to remember the last thing he said to you on Sunday. I don't know what it was, but you're to remember it.'

Peter Furneaux's expression moderated a little. Grundy moved towards him, pad and pencil at the ready, but Barrett pushed himself between them.

'Leave him alone,' he said loudly. 'I'll give you all you want in a minute. Let's go.'

'I'll want quite a lot.' Grundy fell into step alongside. 'I thought this bloke had been put through the wringer and cleared.'

'So he had. We were dead sure he was out of it.'

'What's all this about, then?'

'Wait till we're shot of the world and his wife.'

Near the beginning of the cinder path, Barrett looked back. There was no one on the courts now; no one was sitting down; no one was doing what he had been doing two minutes earlier. The crowd looked and sounded like a crowd urgently seeking a decision, but, of course, whatever decision they took, if any, would make no difference.

'All right,' said Barrett to Grundy. 'There's fresh evidence, see. That hairdresser's next to Furneaux's office, a girl in the back room on the top floor looks out of the window and there's Furneaux coming out the back door of his office. He goes down to the river and she loses sight of him. Well, he wasn't going fishing. There's a cat-walk through that culvert under the road that takes you straight on to the river-path. The time fits exactly.'

Grundy gave a questing sniff. 'When did you find this out?'

'This morning.'

'Why didn't she come forward before? There's been plenty of appeals for witnesses—I know that.'

'She was with the hairdresser bloke, and her husband thinks she was having tea with her aunt in Balham. It took a week for the hairdresser to convince her we'd treat it confidential. Which we are. Same as you're going to. And don't you forget the whole thing's ——'

'Sub judice. Don't tell me that. It's amazing what you can slip past if you know how to do it. And in the trade we know how to do it.' Grundy laughed, showing a collection of remarkably variegated teeth. 'That the lot?'

'All for now, but there'll be more in a day or two. You'll get it.'

'Well, you've already given me enough to make my fortune. Thanks a million, old boy.'

'Don't mention it, old chap. We're all public servants, aren't we?'

'That's right. Thanks, Inspector,' added Grundy, for they stood now, had been standing for nearly half a minute, by the police car, in which Furneaux and Hawkins already sat.

Knightley nodded an acknowledgment. He had shown no impatience at Barrett's having, to an extent, delayed the general departure, perhaps on the argument that it would be better to see the back of Grundy now than to have him all over again down at the station—for the inspector, a supernatural feat of reasoning. Anyway, Grundy took himself off and Barrett climbed in beside the still silent and immobile prisoner.

'Who was there?' Colonel Manton asked Barrett later. 'Who that we're interested in, I mean.'

Barrett told him.

'Oh well, it'll be on everybody's breakfast-table tomorrow. How did young Furneaux take it?'

'Well, he didn't what you'd call jump for joy, sir.'

'Pfui. Try again.'

'Sorry, sir. I gave him your message, and he understood it all right, and it made some difference to him, but I wouldn't like to say how much.'

'Neither should I. I wish I could do something, only I can't think what it might be. Have some whisky. You've earned it.'

'Well, thank you, sir. Just a small one.'

'That letter, the anonymous one. Remarkable piece of mistiming. Wasn't it? You know, my dear Barrett, it's the thought of people's responses to what they'll see on their tea-tables that fascinates me just as much as the other.'

'Their tea-tables, sir?'

'Their high-tea-tables, if you prefer. *Barrett*, you must ... No, I'm sorry, perhaps that was unnecessarily ——'

'You mean the evening papers.'

'I do. I do.'

The following day, the evening papers announced that Capt. W. D. Furneaux, 44, charged with the Riverside Villas murder, had been remanded in custody for a medical report.

XII

A Reconstruction and a Construction

It was half-past eight on the morning of the following Saturday. The streets were still soaked in rain after a violent thunderstorm the previous night: shallow pools on the roadway, individual drops on the aubretia, the lupins, the delphiniums in the little front gardens. These sparkled in the sun, and vapour had already begun to stream upwards from the western sides of the red-tiled roofs. But more thunder was forecast, a bank of light-grey cloud with darker streaks advanced almost imperceptibly from the London direction, and the air felt thick and heavy.

It certainly felt like that to Barrett, not perhaps the best of judges, having been up for nearly two hours already and feeling worried and despondent. As he had done at the same time on the two preceding days, he got out of the police car, knocked at his superior's door and was shown in by Mrs Ellington. He was still no nearer finding out what was the attraction her name held for the colonel, which rankled progressively as his life seemed to come more and more to consist of being no nearer finding out things.

The colonel was having breakfast in what he called his breakfast-room. Put like that it sounded reasonable enough, even pedestrian; but could he mean he never did anything else but have breakfast in it? Was there an elevenses-room, a late-night-snack-room, a gin-and-lime-room? Well, he had the space for them.

'Good morning, Barrett. Great storm last night, it seems. I slept through it; did you?'

'Morning, sir. I think I would have done, but the wife woke me up—scared, she said. Then one of the nippers starts yowling ... '

'You can see there are advantages in celibacy. Negative ones on the whole, I admit. Some coffee?'

On the Thursday, Barrett had been offered, and had declined, a whole breakfast with everything from porridge to cheese (yes, cheese), enough for a mountaineer; but he had accepted coffee because the absurdity of drinking it at such a time was rather enjoyable, as much as if it had been Oxo or a pint of mild. The coffee came out of a silver pot, the cream was in a silver jug, the sugar in a silver bowl. Probably the old boy sat on a silver seat to do his duty.

'There we are. I see there's been trouble in —— What on earth am I saying? I mean Verity's taken his hundredth wicket of the season. No harm in that, surely. I gather you've no news.'

'You gather correct, sir.'

Colonel Manton finished his triangle of toast and Oxford marmalade and lighted a cigarette. He wore a quilted dressing-gown in light-grey silk with lemon-yellow revers, like someone on the stage. But, again like someone on the stage, he would very soon, Barrett knew from experience, vanish and reappear dressed to go out after what seemed like seconds. Now he picked up a couple of newspaper clippings that lay by his plate.

'I have to admit our friend Grundy couldn't have done us prouder. New evidence ... movements on the fatal afternoon ... didn't come forward for personal reasons ... treated as confidential ... medical report ... exact nature and extent of war injury ... significant result ... sensational developments ... within the next few days. Oh, Barrett, what have we done wrong? I should say, what have I done wrong. Have I your support still?'

'My support, of course, sir. That is, I'll never say a word against you. But I'm wondering whether we were right. I mean we. In our deductions.'

'Oh dear, that is depressing. Do you think Cox is right in his?'

'I ... honestly don't know, sir.'

'I do. He isn't. There are no cases on record of people like Cox being right. It's an established rule. One comes across it all the time. Where is he this morning?'

'In bed, if he's got any sense.' Barrett felt almost smug at having got into half a dozen words so much of his attitude to not being in bed himself. 'Taken himself off duty till this evening. Going to buy his wife a hat, he was saying.'

'She deserves one the size of the Crystal Palace, poor soul. I must say I rather care for this freedom of movement he's taken to going in for. The next time I see him, I must remember to lay it down quite unequivocally that the one place we can be dead certain of finding no evidence is New South Wales. We must go. Tell your driver to get down there straight away and we'll join him. I'll meet you outside.'

The colonel bustled off, reappearing to Barrett's view before the police car was out of sight. He now wore a green-and-brown-check suit with a highly suspect matching cap, a combination that suggested a bookie thinly disguised as Sherlock Holmes, or the other way round. He showed Barrett some of his square teeth and said,

'Be sure to let me know at once if you spot anybody

with a squint or a limp or a withered arm. Or even the merest trace of a sinister Chinaman.'

Barrett laughed, taking himself by surprise. Colonel Manton's expression grew stern.

'Don't you know you're not supposed to do that? What's happened to your sense of style? Eh? All right, you're forgiven this once. But don't let anything of the sort occur again.'

Neither spoke for the first minutes of the drive. Then the colonel said,

'Are you anxious?'

'Yes, sir.'

'So am I. We have reason to be. If we don't get results from this I'm afraid we must consider ourselves done for. At least I'll be done for. You'll just have been obeying my orders.'

'Nobody'll hear that from me, sir.'

'I don't greatly care for foreigners, do you? Continentals? And, just between ourselves, I'm not over-fond of the Scotch and the Welsh and the Irish. No, the only people I really like are the English.'

Barrett waited until it seemed more than likely that the other had reached the end of this puzzling train of thought; then, choosing his words carefully, he said, 'Sir: don't you think this project is a little bizarre?'

'Oh, more than a little. It has to be, if our deductions about character are anywhere near the mark. You mean you're embarrassed by what you imagine the others will be thinking.'

'That's right, sir.'

'I remember the R.Q.M.S. in my old battalion had a most expressive phrase he always brought out in situations of this general kind. When it was a matter of, as it might be, incurring the disapproval of people who had no way of bringing their disapproval to bear. Fuck 'em, he used to say. Very telling, don't you think? All these years it's stuck in my mind.'

After that there was more silence until the Jaguar had pulled up on the grass of the Meadow, the fourth car to reach the spot. Standing in a small, rather self-conscious group were Knightley, Duke, Hawkins, another P.C. holding a coil of rope, and the two drivers, and a little way off there was a larger and quite uninhibited group of spectators, mostly children. Faces could be seen through a number of windows. Grundy and a couple of colleagues were hanging about an unexpectedly longer way off.

'Now don't forget, Barrett, the effect to aim for is an unhurried, unruffled dignity thinly veiling the remorselessness presented by a disciplined and infinitely resourceful organization as it marches inexorably towards its goal. Can you manage that, do you suppose?'

'Oh, I reckon so, sir. Have a right good shot at it, anyhow.'

Barrett spoke with the studied normality he had been trained to use when dealing with the mentally disturbed and the violent, but his hopes of calming the colonel down thereby came to nothing. The latter, hands clasped behind back, top half canted forward at something like thirty degrees, was bearing down on the inspector in a way only slightly more remorseless than it was unhurried, inexorable, etc.; that was saying something, though. There was nothing to do bar go along, and feel foolish.

The uniformed men came to attention and the inspector saluted. 'Good morning, Colonel Manton.'

'Good morning to you, Knightley. How long have you and your party been here?'

'Ten, twelve minutes, sir.'

'Excellent.'

With a satisfied nod, the colonel set about lighting a cigarette. Now it was his glance that was unruffled as he viewed the scene with eyes that nevertheless seemed to be standing rather further out of his head than usual.

'Should we be making a start, sir?'

'In due course, Knightley. A word with you first, if I may.'

The two set off side by side down the Meadow, reminding Barrett of a pair of supposed schoolmasters he had once seen in a film. With mortar-boards and gowns on, they had paced a lawn outside a chapel. P.C. Hawkins started to move over towards him, but Barrett could hear inside his head a rustic voice asking a question about what old colonel be thinking he be up to now, then, so he sent Hawkins a glare that brought him up short and was to earn him a subsequent apology.

The perambulation ended. Colonel Manton signed to Barrett and led him off towards the line of villas that lay nearer the river, to the front door of No. 19. This was swung open before either had had the chance to knock on it. The Furneaux boy, in grey flannel shorts and a white shirt with rolled-up sleeves, waited for them inside the threshold.

'What do you want?' he asked. His tone was not friendly, but he seemed (to Barrett) not so much hostile as troubled and bewildered.

'Is your mother at home?'

'No. No, sir. She's at the shops.'

'May we come in?'

'I suppose so. Yes, come in.'

They stood in the sitting-room among leather-covered

furniture and what Barrett considered to be depressingly old-fashioned knick-knacks. None as yet made any move towards a chair. The boy said,

'How's my father? You told me you knew he didn't do it.'

'Your father is being looked after. I also told you that I spoke the truth to you that afternoon. I still ——'

'What's all this fresh evidence stuff I've been reading in the paper?'

'You'll have to trust me about that, about your father's case and about everything to do with this entire affair.'

'How can I?' It was an appeal.

'The colonel's on the level, son,' said Barrett as pre-arranged; it was distasteful, but it had to be done. 'Look, I got kids of my own, though they're not your size yet. Do you think I'd be here now if this wasn't straight?'

'No, all right. But you can't have brought all these policemen round just to show me I can trust you.'

Colonel Manton grinned slightly. 'No, that would hardly impress you one way or the other. May we sit down?'

'Oh yes, sir, sorry.'

'I said I might need your help again. I now do. There's an important fact, or rather possibility, that needs to be decisively established. It won't tell against your father—you have my word for that, which is as much as I can offer you. Is it enough?'

The boy glanced at Barrett. 'Yes, sir.'

'Thank you, Peter. Now I want you to consider this quite coldly, as if you were a lawyer, a barrister. It's medically possible that, after being dealt the fatal blow, Inman fell or was pushed into the river near the bridge, floated downstream in a semi-conscious state until he was near the back-garden gate of this house, emerged there, encountered you and was able to speak a few words before expiring. Highly unlikely, the doctor says, but possible: there are just a few comparable cases.

'But what's medically possible may not have been physically possible in its earlier stages. In other words, we must prove that somebody could have drifted down the river, in no condition to extricate himself at any previous point, but without coming across either any sort of pool where he might have lingered and drowned, or a shallow patch where he might have been caught and held and, I suppose, in the end, also have drowned. Or anything comparable. You follow me so far.'

'Yes, sir.'

'Ocular inspection suggests that that was perfectly feasible. But ocular inspection isn't enough. We must try to repeat Inman's journey with an actual person. And that person—only, of course, with your full and free consent—is going to be you. You—if you agree— are going to enact Inman's part in his watery progress. It'll be a cold and cheerless experience, but not such as to take serious toll of a lad in your ... obviously abundant state of health. No danger involved.'

'I can see why you want to do this experiment, sir, but what I can't see is why me. I mean, there must be hundreds of people you could get to ——'

'My power doesn't extend to hundreds of people in the sense you mean. As you'll see if you consider. The first reason why it has to be you is that it has to be some-body. That sort of reason is the sort of reason behind a great part of human affairs, as I learned some twenty years ago. But to you I must proffer a better reason. A more immediate reason. I have two, in fact. The first is essential. You are about the same weight and general shape as Inman, a qualification not shared by anybody under my control. Policemen are large persons. The second reason is contingent but substantial. I can trust you absolutely to keep quiet about the purpose of what you accurately call the experiment. Except, I suppose, to your mother. But you must have developed your own ways of enjoining silence upon her. Will you do as I ask, Peter? You have a bathing costume, swimming trunks, something of that description whatever it's called?'

'Yes, sir,' said the boy again, but evidently in answer to the second question only. He seemed to be trying to frame a question of his own.

'Only take a few minutes,' put in Barrett. 'We've got a bloke outside now with a rope for you to cling on to.'

'Won't the water-level have risen after the storm last night? So I could float in places where perhaps he couldn't have?'

'It won't affect conditions unduly.' The colonel was positive. 'The flood will have subsided by now to a large extent, and the level was slightly above normal on the day Inman died.'

Barrett said, 'Mind you, that water will be perishing cold, no doubt about that.'

'I don't care. All right, sir, I'll do it. I'll just nip upstairs and change. Shan't be a minute.'

'Sometimes, Barrett,' said the colonel when they were alone, 'you do show a certain rudimentary working knowledge of humanity. And just as well, because he was on the point of seeing through us. What fun it would have been, explaining why we couldn't use Cox. Now, I think, a move to the doorstep.'

Here, within what was in fact very little more than a

minute, Peter Furneaux joined them. He wore a navy-blue pair of Jantzen trunks, white gym shoes and a towel round his shoulders.

'Aren't we going out the back way?'

'Most certainly not; I wouldn't hear of it. Just imagine what four pairs of muddy police boots tramping there and back through the house would do to the carpets. My own dear mother would have put me on skilly for a week if such a frightful thought had even crossed my mind. This way's no further, after all.'

The men in uniform were approaching, and in a few moments the whole party of six men and a boy had rounded the front of No. 21 and reached the riverside path. They were followed at a respectful, almost obsequious, distance by the three journalists, who were holding back out of fear of getting in the way, perhaps, or because Knightley had told them earlier that any closer approach would bring their immediate removal.

A heavy, anvil-shaped cloud with a livid base had forced its way across the eastern and southern skies, blotting out the sun and seeming to load the air with moisture; Barrett fancied he caught a flick of lightning near its edge. It was true that the river had subsided to some extent in the previous few hours: above its rapid surface, bands of glutinous mud, made concave in places by the rush of the flood waters, reached almost to the level of the path. The altered light made the place by the bridge appear nothing as distinguished as sinister or even ugly—just altogether insignificant. Even the tulips beyond the further bank looked too dull and obvious to be worth picking.

The fence along the bank had been mended the day after Inman or his killer or whoever it was had broken it; now Colonel Manton broke it again, laughing silently.

'In the interests of the strictest accuracy,' he said, then, 'Right, my boy. I think we'd better have the rope round you, rather than have you cling on to it: you wouldn't float naturally like that.'

He made a loop under the boy's arms and began to fasten the knot somewhere near the breast-bone, doing nothing that any man at this task would not have done, and yet something in his manner, or perhaps no more than the perfectly natural and indeed necessary closeness of the two figures, suddenly put Barrett in mind of what Cox had said to him when crying off this morning's expedition: 'Advancing the investigation my left foot. The only reason the old brown-hatter's fixed this up is so's he can get as near as he can to that pansified kid in the almost-alto-gether.' Barrett felt some disgust with himself at remembering, and a fierce momentary hatred for Cox, but he could not drive that thought away. And, for the twentieth time since he had started his day's work, what they were doing on this river-bank struck him as worse than bizarre: pointless, senseless, useless even for its insane intention.

The colonel stepped back. 'Comfortable? Good. You'd better try the water with your toe.'

'It's not too bad, sir.'

'A bit more slack there. Now you're helpless, virtually unconscious, unable to influence your course at all. In you go.'

The progress down the river began. Furtively, Barrett looked his colleagues over: the inspector watching events with his usual fixity of expression, the sergeant bored if anything, the constable plying the rope assiduously, anxiously, as though he had the king at the other end of it. Hawkins had moved away from the path at a nod from the inspector and was shooing away some onlookers, a job that possibly made more sense than anybody else's. The colonel's eyes were on the boy in the water, but the rest of his face gave no indication whether it might at any moment break into a snarl of lust or a huge yawn. Barrett himself yawned.

Once the Furneaux lad was carried against the far bank, once he drifted into some reeds, once he went aground on a pebbly shelf, but each time the force of the current swung him free again. Within a very few minutes he and the rest of the party had reached the end of their journey, outside the back gate of No. 19 Riverside Villas.

Colonel Manton smiled. He might have been congratulating himself on having brought off a chancy practical joke. 'An important possibility confirmed as possible. Very good, Peter: you can come out now.'

The P.C. stooped to lend a hand, but the boy showed no disposition to leave the water. He seemed to be staring at a point in the river-bank immediately in front of him. Then he reached out and made tugging, twisting motions, as if trying to free some object embedded there, and very soon it became clear that that was just what he was about. Without speaking, he held up above his head a silvery thing about a foot long, a thinnish cylinder unequally tapered. Barrett found himself thinking it ought to be gold, not silver. Why? Because it reminded him of the rungs connecting the legs of the gold-painted chairs at the Locarno dance-hall in Streatham, where he sometimes took his wife on a Saturday evening.

'Where exactly did you find that?' asked the colonel, reaching down.

'It was sticking out of the bank,' said the boy, indistinctly because he had begun to shiver. 'Where it looks as if some mud's been washed away.'

'You're cold ... '

In a moment, Peter Furneaux stood on the bank with his towel round his shoulders, but shaking violently. 'Water ... freezing ... worse than you think ... '

'You get into the house and soak in a hot bath,' said the colonel. 'I'll be in touch with you later. Thank you for all you've done. Cut along.'

More closely examined, what the boy had found proved to consist of painted wood, to have in it a couple of empty screw-holes and an L-shaped metal hook, to be slitted or split at its narrower end, to carry a short blunt metal spike at its broader.

'Christ!' said Barrett in an explosive stage-whisper.

'Indeed.'

'You were expecting to find it?'

'I wasn't expecting ... ' The colonel noticed the closer approach of the inspector and the sergeant, and went on in a different tone, ' ... to find it just where it was, but it was obvious to me that it would have to have been somewhere in this part of the area. I mean, it absolutely stares one in the face, I should have thought.'

There was an admiring silence. Knightley said,

'What exactly is it, sir?'

'It's several things, my good inspector. For one, it's manufactured. For another, it's vital evidence. Take it with you now and keep it out of sight. Barrett and I will join you over by the cars in a minute or two.'

After the necessary interval, Barrett said, 'Had you really any idea it was there, sir? You can tell me, you know.'

'What are you talking about? Of course I knew it was there. No, of course I had no idea anything was anywhere in particular. Manufactured, yes; vital evidence, most certainly; but, more yet, it's a gift from the gods. Until a few hours ago, the minutest inspection possible, or at least practicable, would have failed to detect any sign of its presence. And we choose this moment to come by on a quite different errand. It's enough to make one jolly well want to fling oneself down on one's knees in gratitude. Our next move is not far to seek. First … '

Barrett got down nearly to his knees, not in gratitude but to pursue an irrelevant question that had come to his mind. He reached out and dipped his fingers into the water. It was indeed very far from warm, but not too bad—exactly how the Furneaux boy had first described it. Still, after spending several minutes more or less completely immersed …

XIII

The Final Assault

For most of that day Peter found himself unable to think
—think in the sense of move from one idea to another.
There was only one idea in his mind, and he could not
move from it in any direction, and it would not go away.
It stayed there while he told his mother, on her return
from the shops, something of what he and the police had
been engaged in during her absence, while she responded
one after the other with incredulity, indignation, baffle-
ment leading to a diminished incredulity, while she came
to lose interest in the topic and set about developing, or
recapitulating, themes of dread and despair and power-
lessness in the face of the arrest, while, in effect unheard,
he repeated what he had said a dozen times before about
the whole thing being a blind, aimed at making the real
criminal feel falsely secure and give himself away. She
cried a little and he tried to comfort her, tried too to feel
sorry for her and failed, not because she struck him as
not worth feeling sorry for, but because nothing could
strike him, or rather because that one idea struck him every
minute.

He tried to read, and found, as he came to each phrase
in turn, that he had forgotten the one before; even the
eagerly awaited last episode of the Roy Vickers serial, which
he had been following in the *Daily Mirror*, meant nothing
whatever to him and had to be put aside until his literacy
should return, if it ever did. The mere prospect of listening to the gramophone or the wireless was boring to the

point of repulsion; perhaps he had never really enjoyed either in the past, only fancied he had. From behind the set of *The Children's Encyclopaedia* in his bedroom, he pulled out his small and unselect hoard of offensive material, chiefly magazine photographs of girls in bathing dresses and very incompetent drawings of girls with no clothes on, together with manuscript versions of *The Good Ship Venus* and other such works, laboriously transcribed in breaks and lunch-hours from Forester's master-copies; all of it fully as stirring now as a set of Happy Families. He telephoned Reg, not with anything practical in mind but, for once, just to see him and chat to him; a voice probably belonging to Betty, the dud maidservant, said that Master Reggie had gone out in the car with his mother and father and had not said when he would be back.

Lunch was boiled cod and parsley sauce, never a favourite dish. Today, eating a warm, slightly dampened copy of the *Radio Times* might have been more difficult. But Peter's mother could not manage more than a couple of mouthfuls herself, and perhaps thought it unfair to go on at him to eat up, or else just failed to notice he had not. Both got some tinned mandarin oranges down, and then he made some tea which neither drank.

Up in his room again, he felt a headache coming on. That was good: it tended to reduce the pressure of the idea in his mind; he made no move towards the aspirin in the bathroom cupboard. There was more thunder on the way. A faint rumble drew him to the window, from which his eyes took in the rolls and bulges of dark cloud covering the sky, the muddy garden, the stretches of fencing, the trees that looked like masses of seaweed on poles. Thundery weather gave you headaches, and when the storm broke and the rain came it cleared the air and your headache went. So the longer it took for the storm to break the better. He rested his forehead against the pane, but the glass seemed moist and tepid, either because it really was or because his forehead was not as hot as it felt to him. Perhaps this was what it was like when people had angina pectoris and the doctor gave them six months to live: always the same whatever they did and wherever they went. He rebuked himself for comparing his own state to something to do with death, but then there was death too in what was in his mind.

It must have been about five o'clock that somebody knocked at the front door. When Peter and his mother went and answered it together—a habit they had grown into over the days since the arrest—they found Mr Hodgson there. It was obvious from the miniature bow he made, and the way he wanted something to fiddle with, that he had been sent rather than come of his own accord, but when he spoke it was just as obvious that he was in favour of what he was saying.

'Good afternoon, Mrs Furneaux. Hallo, Peter. The wife and I were thinking, we thought it must be a bit depressing for you over here all on your own on a Saturday, so we thought you might care to step across the way a bit later on, like round about seven, and have a bite to eat with us, nothing fancy, just what we'd be having ourselves anyway, and then maybe listen-in or play a hand of cards or something of that. Geoff and Daph'll be out,' he went on, briskly putting paid to the first genuine, full-sized new thought Peter had had since that morning, 'and young Cissie'll be on her way to bed, so it'll only just be us four. Well ... '

Mrs Furneaux accepted gratefully, without any hint of

the condescension her son had feared, and, when the door was shut, said with tears in her eyes that it was nice to think some people were human and to find that they, she and he, were not complete outcasts after all. The implication of this was far from the strict truth: since that Tuesday, a dozen neighbours had called at the house, some more than once, and more than a dozen others had telephoned, but none had been able to come up with more than asking if there was anything they could do, and, of course, there was nothing. Or rather, there was nothing that would not have been much too much like visiting the sick when you had not actually got to. Peter's uncle and aunt on his father's side had come down from Denmark Hill to spend the Thursday and the Friday, promising to return on the Monday. Although they clearly meant well, it had been hard work not just listening to their laments and protests, but sort of standing in for the police, being asked bitterly how he would like that kind of treatment, told threateningly that somebody was going to pay for this. The only real help had been a short visit from Mr Taylor. He had been quite positive that everybody at the Grammar understood the position, and that Peter could not be expected to turn up there again while the present circumstances lasted. He had also been pretty stern and detailed about the reading and the written work Peter must do at home so as to keep up with the others, just stern and detailed enough to forestall any weeping.

Between Mr Hodgson's invitation and its being taken up, only one thing of any importance happened, but it was especially important to Peter. The evening paper arrived, carrying low down on its front page a report that police had reconstructed part of the circumstances of the Inman murder. A few details were given, but there was no mention of the silver object found in the bank of the river. There would not be, Peter told himself at once; that was exactly what Colonel Manton would have seen to it that there should not be. Of course, of course—and yet in some way the idea that had been with him all these hours was changed in meaning by the omission: from being something he must face but could not face, it became something he must do but could not do.

In the manner of one obeying perforce a hypnotic command earlier implanted, he washed his armpits and slapped into them some of his mother's talcum powder, put on a clean shirt and a pair of long trousers, gave his hair a good brushing—he could not be absolutely certain, just ninety-nine point nine recurring per cent certain, that Daphne might not be present for a few seconds before she went wherever whoever the hell it was was taking her out or after he brought her back.

After a couple of weeks' worth of hanging about, seven o'clock arrived. Peter and his mother went round the edge of the Meadow (rather than walk straight across it and get soaked halfway to the knee) and pitched up at the Hodgsons'. They were shown into the sitting-room at the front of the house. Daphne was nowhere to be seen, nor, for that matter, was Geoff. Mrs Furneaux accepted a glass of gin and it—it? it? This it could not be the same it that Clara Bow on the films had, or had had, nor could they be linked by the first it giving you the second it, which nobody's mother had, or could have had. Most likely the it now on show was nothing more than some mostly fictitious substance, perhaps oriental in theory like the secret ingedient in the face-cream advert that stopped women ever growing old, and probably consisting in practice of coloured smelly water.

It, it was plain, was for ladies only. Mrs Hodgson had some with her gin, but Peter got a glass of cider, and Mr Hodgson, after pouring the last of a quart beer bottle into his own glass, filled it up with more of the same from another. After a silence, Mrs Hodgson opened a discussion about the weather, which certainly deserved it. At the moment, with the curtains left undrawn, a premature dusk showed through the panes, and, in the minutes that followed, thunder twice rippled in the distance. Peter's headache throbbed. There was supper in the dining-room, and he at once forgot what they had eaten, but took in something of their surroundings. From the way his parents, especially his father, were in the habit of going on about the Hodgsons and their way of life, he had been prepared for newspapers as a tablecloth and sawdust on the floor; in fact, there was a good deal of lace, serviettes in bone rings and artificial flowers. Back in the sitting-room, he noticed an eighteen-inch-high figure in full armour guarding the empty tiled grate, and, on the lilac-distempered walls, gilt-framed pictures of Arabian scenes, with camels, palms and pyramids against several sunsets.

The wireless was turned on and listened to for a space Peter could not measure, nor could he afterwards remember what had been broadcast: he was back with his headache and his idea. In the end, Mr Hodgson switched off, poured himself more beer and said,

'We might as well talk about it. No point in not. Better if we do.'

'Oh, I really don't know,' said his wife.

'Course it's better, love. All right, but we got two intelligent human beings here. You stop me if you want, Mrs Furneaux. And you, Pete. The way I look at it is this, and I seen these rozzers at work—I been one myself,

for lord's sake. When they want to get someone, they
don't give a, a damn how they sets about it or what trouble
they puts people to. All right. You been to see the captain,
right, Mrs Furneaux? He say anything? Anything more
than they're treating him okay, no complaints kind of
style?'

'No, very little more.' The answer came in an accent
designed (Peter guessed despondently) to rebuke the one
in which the questions had been put, but otherwise it
sounded genuine. 'Captain Furneaux was extremely
reticent.'

'I'm sure. And the solicitor isn't saying anything neither.
For why? Because that's the way they fixed it. All a put-
up job. What I'm saying, he's collaborating with 'em, the
captain is, I know, I can feel it. They got some scheme
going. He's not guilty, not in a million years. It's all a
trick. You heard how this fellow Evans rung me up the
day it happened?' (Peter mentally agreed, with some
surprise, that indeed they had heard, everybody had heard,
as much and a great deal more.) 'Well, Evans done it,
that's obvious. And I'd swear on the book that whoever
it was whose voice I heard over the phone that time, it
wasn't the captain's. Not ever. Don't you worry, I don't
know what they're up to, and I reckon they're exceeding
their authority arresting him, but it's not because they
think he's guilty. Part of some scheme, that's what it is.

'Now, that's cleared the air. Let's have a few hands to
pass the time. You all right for a bit of solo, Pete?'

Peter said truthfully that he found whist rather complicated, so rummy was settled on. Mr Hodgson got the
cards out, arranged the seating, refilled his glass with
beer and dealt. As time went by, he took off his jacket,
then, in the face of looks from his wife and the absence

of them from Mrs Furneaux, his collar and tie. It was certainly hot in the little sitting-room. Thunder sounded again, moving closer. The play continued, with Peter just able to sustain his attention through each hand. Finally there was rain, and lightning, and thunder in earnest, and Mr Hodgson shut the windows, but left the curtains undrawn so as not to keep out what air there was.

A few minutes after that there was a knock at the door. It was Daphne, very much accompanied by the tall swine who had been squiring her at the dance a fortnight earlier. They had hardly looked into the sitting-room, and Daphne had hardly glanced at Peter and away again, before they went off to dry themselves, though most parts of them appeared dry enough. Mrs Furneaux made motions towards leaving, but was restrained.

'You can't go in this,' said Mr Hodgson. 'Let's have a last cup of tea, eh, love? I'll put the kettle on.'

The card game broke up. Peter went to the window, most of which reflected the brightly lit room behind him, but he could make out something of what lay within his silhouette. Not much: it was not yet officially dark, so to speak, but, except at the instant of a lightning-flash, heavy cloud and thick, drifting rain would have made it very hard to see anyone who might have been fool enough to be standing or walking on the Meadow. Peter saw nobody. Suddenly he saw nothing at all, stared into space as it dawned on him that he must move now, go and telephone Colonel Manton and tell him what he knew, do it from here, because here he could make the call without his mother listening and at home he could not.

He asked permission from Mr Hodgson, who had come back into the room, got it and was out in the hall before his mother had time to question or object. He opened the local directory to find the colonel's number. Just then, Daphne came down the stairs.

'Hallo,' he said, reckoning that a few seconds' delay would make no odds. 'Had a nice evening?'

'All right.'

'What evenings next week are you free?'

'Don't know.'

She was moving past him towards the sitting-room door. He had a tiny moment to think of something more to say. Before it had elapsed, his keen ears picked out a sound from among the rushing of the rain, or rather two sounds: a sharp thud as of some object striking the front outside wall of the house, and then a brief movement on the Meadow near by.

'What was that?' he asked.

'What? What was what?'

'I heard something out there.'

'Get away,' she said above a piercing crackle of thunder. 'It's as quiet as the grave from where I am.'

'I really did.'

Daphne did not bother to answer this feeble attempt to prolong a feeble ruse. She went away. Peter turned pages. He knew now that the first sound had reminded him of a fives ball hitting the wall of the court. Manton, Col. R. P. W. ... 8. Just 8. Pretty grand, that.

He reached for the receiver, but never touched it. There was a loud smash and a loud jangling noise and an assorted outcry from the sitting-room. Peter ran in. An irregularly shaped part of the mirror formed by the uncurtained windows was missing. Fragments of glass lay on the floor below them. All were on their feet, still exclaiming, Mr Hodgson swearing loudly and moving to the window. Peter put his arm round his mother's shoulders. He caught sight of a small whiteish sphere slowly coming to rest in a far corner. Then it was a fives ball, and the previous shot had ... No—a golf ball.

'You bloody kids!' bawled Mr Hodgson into the darkness. 'What do you think you're playing at? Might have put someone's eye out.' He looked over his shoulder. 'I'm going to take a stick to 'em. Daph, get me the torch. Middle drawer in the kitchen.'

Daphne, seemingly toned up by the novelty, hurried out. Peter joined Mr Hodgson at the window.

'Little swine. Must be off their bloody heads. I'll ——'

He stopped speaking as somebody flashing a torch ran into view and stopped near the garden gate. A man's voice called,

'What's going on here?'

'Had my front window broken, look. Must be a gang of ——'

Another missile crashed through a pane at the far end of the window, missing Peter by a yard and scattering more glass. Outside, the torch-beam swept to and fro, but revealed nothing and nobody. There was the sound of a police whistle, and the owner of the torch began running across the Meadow. At the same time, more torch-beams, three or four of them, came into being diagonally opposite and moved jerkily from left to right. While Mr Hodgson bellowed for Daphne and the two women competed in shock and distress, Peter slipped out into the hall. Trembling, he bent and tucked his turn-ups into the tops of his socks, and opened the front door and left it open and was away.

The rain drove hard, both forcefully and like innumerable solid particles, into his face. He stumbled twice in ten yards, the second time going down on hands and knees, but was able to keep the torch-beams in sight—they were nearly opposite him now. In a brief flare of lightning, he saw dark waterproof capes glistening with wet and the unmistakable rounded shape of a police helmet. The thunder came almost at once, a frenzy of continuous bangs that carried the physical resilience of the skin of a pounded drum. He was already soaked quite through, and the going was so rough in the darkness that he had to slacken his pace. Ahead, the torches, or those holding them, had split into two groups, one apparently halted, the other still on the move in the same direction as before. Peter hesitated, then turned a little aside and made after the second party. In a few seconds this too halted, or hesitated, before plunging on afresh—he guessed along the river-path in the direction away from the town and towards the road-bridge. Gasping, knuckling rain out of his eyes, he followed.

By now he could tell darker shapes from lighter and had his bearings, but lost it all when a torch was switched on straight into his face from a dozen feet away.

'Halt! Where d'you think you're——? Ah, it's all right, sonny. P.C. Hawkins.' The light shifted to prove this was so before being turned off. 'Don't you be scared, now. Everything's nicely under control. But what's got you out here in this?'

'Saw the torches and ... '

'It's all right, boy. You'd best be getting into the dry and give yourself a good towelling or you catch cold. You're not as wet as I am, mind. I been in the river, I have.' P.C. Hawkins spoke as if to a frightened child. 'Yes, I got a fine old butt in the tummy and in I went. Bit of luck, I dropped my torch on the bank, and it were still going when I ... Hey!'

Another torch swung towards them; it was Mr Hodgson.

While he and the constable were exchanging questions, Peter took himself off. When he was clear, he stopped to get his breath back. If he was right in what he had surmised while running across the Meadow, there was no hurry for the moment, and if he was wrong there was none at all. He found his breath would not come back, not all of it all the way. Even after his heart had stopped banging at his chest, he still gasped shallowly and irregularly. The lightning flashed and he shut his eyes until the thunder had finished sounding—further off now. When he opened his eyes he could see a little, enough to find his way to where he wanted to go. The rain seemed to have lessened, though it still swayed and drove hither and thither. He set off down the river-bank towards the town with the river swirling noisily beside him.

He thought to himself that he never wanted to see another scary film or read another scary book for the rest of his life. None of the ones he had seen and read so far were any good at all, and he knew now that none of the others could be either. Such things were not just feeble imitations of what they were supposed to be about, any more than a car was an imitation horse—they both moved, that was all. Films and books happened outside you. So, presumably, did poems and records, which must mean that they were no good either. Perhaps being grown-up was just like being fourteen, only you had a job and money and a wife and children, which would not make any difference to what happened inside you.

Here was the culvert, and the street-lamp burning near it gave him some real help as he lowered himself from the bank. Which side was the cat-walk? If it was the other side ... No, it must be this side, because the path was this side. There, hardly at all above the surface of the water, which was natural on a night like this. He got one foot firmly on to it, found a metal hand-hold on the brickwork, pushed himself cautiously backwards until he could slide his other foot into position, searched blind until he found another hand-hold, and was inside the mouth of the culvert. Here it was very dark and the river made a lot of noise, but he had no time to take any of this in, because there was somebody else in the culvert, as he had expected. The other person promptly struck at him with a knife (he felt the tearing of his shirt-sleeve and the stinging pain along the fleshy part of his forearm), which he had not expected. Chance or instinct enabled him to grab the wrist above the hand that held the knife, but in doing so he lost his balance on the narrow cat-walk, and within a second he and his adversary were in the water together.

XIV

How Can They Prove It?

There followed what seemed a long struggle. Some of it was a sort of fight—he held off all attempts to detach his hand from that wrist—some was a constant effort to breathe or not to start drowning, and the rest was a mere flurry of limbs to avoid being helplessly swept away. Then there was a bump; the water became shallower and less disturbed; both pairs of feet found bottom at the same moment. The hand with the knife in it was torn free.

'Don't—it's me—it's Peter.'

All resistance ceased at once. Peter realized that he and the other had been carried through the culvert and some way further, to a point inside a bend where the bank jutted out. He could hear the rain, but not feel it, and not see it until he looked back the way they had come, where tall veils of it swung slowly to and fro in the light of the street-lamp.

'Oh God,' said Mrs Trevelyan. 'How badly have I hurt you?'

'See, it's just a scratch. It's all right.'

'I didn't think of it being you. I'm sorry, I didn't mean it.'

'It's all right.'

'I'm sorry. How did you know I was there?'

'Because I know you. It was where you'd go where they wouldn't look and you could work out what to do next. Let's ...'

He half climbed, half rolled himself out of the water

and helped Mrs Trevelyan to follow him. They crouched side by side among beaten-down weeds and clumps of coarse grass. There was nowhere to shelter and no need now anyway.

'We'd better be getting back,' said Peter.

'What for? They'll know it wasn't your father now.'

'You've got to give yourself up. They'll soon catch you if you don't.'

'No they won't. I've got it all worked out. I know the South Downs well: I was born in Worthing and I used to go for long rambles. I could hide there until they stop looking for me. The weather's bound to get better soon.'

Peter stared at the face he could not see. 'But what about food?'

'I'd steal from farms. And there are berries and things.'

'How do you think you could get there? They'll be circulating a description of you now and your picture will be in all the papers in the morning. And you're all wet, and you'd never ——'

'I'll break into shops and get fresh clothes and money and a pair of spectacles, and I'll do my hair differently. You could come too, and help me and keep me company. It would be so lovely, and such fun. When they'd stopped looking for us, we could change our names and go and live in Wales or somewhere. We could be together for always. Wouldn't you like that?'

A flash of lightning came, a weak one, but bright enough for him to see her face, not wild-eyed and distorted, but with an expression of eager persuasiveness, as if she were trying to talk him out of doing his homework and into playing tennis with her. He said, with difficulty,

'But it can't happen. It's impossible.'

'It can if we want it to. Oh, darling Peter ... '

A wet arm went round his shoulders, wet lips tried to find his, and a hand groped. Peter had not known that a person's mind could hurt as badly as his had started to. He pulled himself away and struggled to get up.

'No! You're insane! And you're bad!'

After a silence, in which thunder was just audible through the noise of the rain and the river, Mrs Trevelyan said in an ordinary voice, 'I suppose I am. It would never have worked, would it? I just got carried away. I don't think I'm insane, but I am bad. I'm sorry.'

Peter was crying, but no one could see. 'Come back with me now and give yourself up. You must. Listen, I know roughly how you did it, and they'll soon find out, I expect, but nobody saw you, did they?'

'No.'

'And does anybody know why you did it? Can they find out?'

'No. I don't think so. No.'

'Then how can they prove it? If you go back and say you lost your head, it'll look that much better for you.'

'All right. You'll have to help me. I feel rather weak.'

With his arm in hers, they set out along the bank and approached the road. A car swished by towards London. The rain was falling off. Peter said,

'Why did you shoot those golf-balls?'

'To show the guilty person was still about, not in prison.'

'I know, you said, but you didn't have to do that.'

'Yes I did. I couldn't bear it because of you. I kept trying to show it wasn't your father, and it wouldn't go right. I attacked him in your hall, and I wanted you or your mother to see me, but you didn't come, and I couldn't wait any longer—I had to get back, and I had to keep quiet, in case someone looked out and saw me going in. So it was only his word.' Mrs Trevelyan spoke in a monotone. 'Then I sent them an anonymous letter, but that could have been him too. I should have waited. Then they arrested him and I thought it must be a trick, and then I saw them using you for that river thing, and I couldn't bear it. That colonel must have guessed that was just the ... '

'Speak more clearly, I can't hear you.'

'Sorry, I seem to be so tired all of a sudden. I had to make them set him free for your sake. My husband's away until the morning. So I rigged up the ... I don't think I can go any further. My legs have gone all ... '

'It's only a few more yards.'

'Then they were waiting for me. Hadn't thought of that. You'll have to hold me up or something.'

Peter did not want to put his arm round her, but he did, and together they made their way to the back gateway on No. 21. Here she stopped, leaned against the fence and said with her face turned away.

'Forgive me, not now, just some time. Don't say anything. I know it looks as if I felt I just had to have you, but I did want to please you as well. Don't say anything. I don't want you to forget me, but you'll have to try to. Anyway, all the women you meet for the rest of your life will be less bad than me. I think I can manage on my own now.'

She led the way up the path and into the kitchen. All the downstairs lights were on, and Constable Barrett was there. He asked them to come with him.

In the dining-room at the front of the house sat Colonel Manton, but what took Peter's attention was a strange contrivance assembled before an open window: a dozen strands of heavy model-aeroplane elastic a yard or more long, one end fastened to the upright of the window-frame, the other to the stout wooden post of a dresser, in the middle a sort of pouch, perhaps of leather, like that of a catapult— in fact, what he was looking at was a catapult, of unusual power, because it could be cranked up to any amount of tension by the clothes-mangle that stood ready to hand, and of unusual accuracy, as was suggested by the long card-board tube, of the sort used to hold maps, that pointed across the window-sill in the direction of the Hodgsons' house.

The colonel took even less notice of Peter than Peter had of him. He rose to his feet and said directly and loudly to Mrs Trevelyan,

'With this apparatus, or a version of it, you propelled at Christopher Inman a lethal weapon constructed from a toy glider.' (So they knew all the time, thought Peter.) 'We have that weapon and we now have its means of launching. You were alone when the fatal injury was inflicted. Your motive was to stop Inman's mouth—I don't care to go further for the moment, but you can see I know what I'm talking about. Your flight confesses your guilt.'

Wearing women's trousers and a shirt of no certain colour, Mrs Trevelyan listened to this. She looked small, young, wretched and very wet, but she spoke with no sign of weakness.

'Nonsense, Colonel Manton. As regards my flight, as you call it, I'd played a silly joke on the Hodgsons and panicked when all your policemen started milling about. As regards the rest of it, I'll say nothing until I have legal representation. And shouldn't you have cautioned me?'

'Very well.' The colonel turned without delay to his assistant. 'Barrett, take this woman into the next room and keep her there. I'll join you shortly.'

'May I have some dry clothes, please?'

'Later. You won't catch cold at this temperature. Go.'

Without looking at Peter, Mrs Trevelyan left with the constable.

'Now: you pursued her and induced her to come back here?'

'Yes, sir.'

'Good. And good work. Now you must go. I'll be in touch at a later stage. Meanwhile, say nothing to anyone. You merely got lost in the dark. Tomorrow you may hear something that will surprise you, but you still say nothing. Your father will be released immediately. Will you be able to sleep?'

'Oh yes, sir, I'm having trouble keeping awake now.'

'Good night, Peter.'

They parted at the front door. Peter saw that his own house was in darkness and the Hodgsons' lighted. He could imagine Mr Hodgson's insistence: Mrs Furneaux was going to be kept company until her son came back where he had started from. That left him free. He let himself into Montrose, hurried through to the back door and, cautiously now, emerged again. He did not feel in the least sleepy, nor did he notice his wet clothing. The colonel's manner, his unusual rapidity of speech, had shown that something urgent, something important was going to happen, surely the something that he, Peter, would be surprised at the next day.

The need for silence slowed him down, but within five minutes of leaving the house next door he was back outside its sitting-room windows, listening hard. The colonel's voice, as on a previous occasion, was easily audible.

'That can cut two ways. An attractive young woman will indeed have the jury on her side if other things are equal, but here they're not. Are they? A depraved and vicious young woman's attractiveness will weigh against her.'

Mrs Trevelyan said something indistinguishable.

'Easily enough, I assure you. That boy will give evidence, and in the course of his examination he'll be asked about his association with you.'

The reply, which was quite long, mentioned a judge, or the judge. From where he was, Peter could not see into the room. To move to a better position might give away his presence, and he did not now want to see. Colonel Manton was speaking again.

'He may or he may not. That depends on his curiosity, among other things. But one question, and the boy's inevitable response to it—I don't mean necessarily in words, merely his demeanour—will be enough. For the rest of his life he'll be somebody who was debauched in youth by a murderess—because even if you get off everyone will know you were guilty. Can you face having that happen to him?'

A question was asked in return.

'What of that, since it's true? I saw the two of you at that dance, but that was only ——'

'You wanted to get your hands on him yourself, you filthy old homo!' said Mrs Trevelyan quite audibly.

'Cut that out, missus, if you please.' That was the detective-constable.

'For one thing, because it wastes time. Any moment now those idiots are going to come crawling back empty-handed, and I'll have to arrest you and take you away, and we'll have lost our chance of doing a deal ... Surely it's obvious? You confess, and then there's no prosecution, no witnesses, no evidence, and nobody knows about the boy. I give you my solemn ——'

'Bluff! Bloody bluff! Cock and balls and bluff!'

'*Madam*: you underestimate me. If you are found not guilty of murder, I'll have you immediately rearrested on a charge of indecent assault, to which you are totally vulnerable. The maximum gaol sentence for that, which in the circumstances is what you'll undoubtedly get, is rather stiff, and the boy will be really famous. Won't he? It's my job to see to it that you pay. By one means or another.

'Mrs Trevelyan, your life is at an end whatever happens. Don't ruin someone else's. Confess! Confess, and save that other life.'

There was a murmur.

'That's no good. Don't you see? You must write it down.' The colonel spoke with immense emphasis. 'And sign it. Don't you understand?'

A very long pause followed, and, for the first and only time, Peter wished he could see into the room.

'Here, missus.'

'I killed … Christopher Inman. Is that enough?'

'Sign it. Thank you. Now I think we could all do with a cup of tea, if you'd be kind enough to make one. Meanwhile I suggest you think over what happened at Christchurch, near Bournemouth, just over a year ago.'

'I already have,' said Mrs Trevelyan.

Peter heard her leave the sitting-room and cross into the kitchen.

'What happened at Christchurch, sir?'

'I'll tell you later. Shush.'

Peter saw the back door, the kitchen door, slowly open and the figure of Mrs Trevelyan slowly step on to the path within five yards of him. The rain had stopped, the sky had lightened faintly and he had a glimpse of her face. It was not as he remembered it even from ten minutes before: all its intelligence and animation were gone. He could not hear her feet on the concrete of the path as, at the same slow pace, almost like someone at a ceremony, she started walking down the little garden. The voices in the room spoke again.

'So she was never here, sir, not after she ran away in the first place.'

'Correct, Barrett. She went straight to where she's going now, leaving her confession for us to find.'

'Were you bluffing?'

'Yes, and she was nearly sure of it, but that wasn't good enough. For her. Considering what was at stake.'

'Who was at stake.'

Mrs Trevelyan reached the garden gate and, without looking back, went out by it and passed from view.

XV

Into a Blue Sky

'I've a number of apologies to offer you, Peter, and some information to impart. An unofficial talk for a change. I thought this arrangement would be suitable.'

This arrangement involved Peter sitting in the Jaguar while Colonel Manton drove him home from school, and had come about after an unexpected summons to the head-master's study as classes were ending for the day. It was nearly a fortnight since the body of Mrs Trevelyan, with five self-inflicted stab-wounds in it, had been found caught against a bush in the river half a mile from where she had lived.

'But first of all,' pursued the colonel as they drove along the Embankment, 'let me say I hope you're well and that Clacton-on-Sea was a success.'

'Oh yes, sir, thank you. We had a very nice week. Lots of sun.'

'Excellent. You can face discussing the obvious questions?'

'I want to get it all cleared up in my mind.'

'Better still. The apologies, then. Chiefly for what I did to your father, and through him to your mother and yourself—harassing him, trumping up false evidence against him, arresting him. I didn't dare tell him the arrest was a fake—I couldn't rely on his powers as an actor.'

'Just as well. No, he understands all that, sir ... '

'But he still feels a little aggrieved, and being arrested for murder, even when clearly innocent, doesn't much advance one's reputation. I may be able to alleviate that. A Sunday newspaper has invited me to write an account of the whole affair. In it, I intend to lay some stress on your father's contribution. It's true he had no choice, but I shan't say that.'

Cutting through the traffic, the car swung left on to Waterloo Bridge. The sun shone brightly on the water, on the shipping, the quays and cranes and warehouses. It all looked not only busy but tremendously varied and complicated, just the bits that showed, the bits you could see, of a whole world all working smoothly away under its own mysterious laws. Across the river, the colonel slipped the Jaguar past a tram on its near side and continued,

'Now the apologies to you. Making you do that infernal floating act. It was designed purely and simply to put moral pressure on the criminal, which it succeeded in doing, as we saw, but of course the ——'

'And as she told me that night.'

'Oh. Interesting. In a way. But, as I was saying, the godsend was your finding the weapon for us. You recognized it at once, didn't you?—even though she'd removed the wing and thrown the rudder and tail-plane away afterwards. It took us some time and thought.'

'I didn't only recognize it, sir. As the fuselage of a six-penny Condor glider, I mean. It told me who the murderer was. Because I'd explained a little about gliders and catapults and aeroplane elastic to her ten days before the murder. I hadn't thought she was listening.'

'But she was. Ah-ha. Hence your fit of the shivers. I see. Do you like cigarettes? You've been through more than most grown-up people have to in a lifetime, so I don't see why you shouldn't have a little grown-up consolation, so to speak. I'll put my case and lighter here, and you can jolly well light up whenever you feel like it.'

Peter took a cigarette. It turned out to be called a Three Castles, which he had never even heard of. As smoked by the crowned heads of Europe and Colonel Manton, D.S.O., M.C. They probably cost about half-a-crown for twenty.

'What was the point of the glider business, sir? Wouldn't lots of other ways have been simpler?'

'Indeed they would. Poison was the obvious way, especially in her situation, but she'd just been reminded of how poison virtually always gets traced to its user by reading—a great reader, that one—by reading about the recent conviction of one Charlotte Bryant for the ——'

'I know about her, sir.'

'Do you? Let me expound. A great slab. Ask questions if desired. From the beginning, then. She'd been having an affair with Inman—a good idea to begin with, less good when her husband was about to be given more money and moved elsewhere. It had all been very discreet, no excursions round the pubs and so on. That must have been her idea: Inman wasn't discreet by nature, as we're aware. Those threats at the dance weren't really malicious; I see them as the expression of a childish love of telling secrets. Anyway, in time he threatened to turn very indiscreet indeed. He was going to tell Trevelyan his big secret, perhaps start divorces going. In fact, his mind was on that while he was dying. As you reported—he had to tell him, a man has a right to know, all that. Yes, let's clear up those dying words, shall we? He heard it. You would hear a thing like that coming at you. In addition, probably, to the noise made by its launching. And then all that hallo business. What was he trying to say? What must that projectile have looked like to him in that instant? You have ten seconds.'

Peter needed only three. 'Arrow.'

'Correct. More exposition. It was obvious we were dealing with a very learned, thoughtful criminal. Her object was to kill her victim in a way that was possible only for a very strong person, a category that excludes women. Therefore a tremendous blow must be delivered in the least vulnerable part of the body. That was the key to the whole case. Why an apparent stab in the cranium? I saw the answer to that straight away, so I had two suspects, her and your unfortunate father, whom she'd overlooked, and whose lack of alibi was a huge snag, the cause of so many of her subsequent difficulties and mistakes—the abortive attack on him and so on. Hodgson, by the way, was never a serious candidate. He could have done it, physically, so he couldn't have done it. And that telephone call from Evans—not Hodgson's style. He's intelligent, but not learned or thoughtful. She had nothing against him: it was just misdirection, a tactic she was too fond of.

'We'd better keep to strict chronology from now on. She'd assembled her contraption and made her missile, but would it penetrate a human skull? No sort of practice target or dummy would throw any light on that question. The answer was to steal Boris Karloff from the museum, leaving as many false clues as possible, and try it on him. Evidently it worked—I should say that some of this is surmise, but it fits the facts, of which there are several to come. She had some days for practice shoots in her garden, secure from observation. On the Tuesday, Inman was coming to see her as usual. She went to the road-bridge, broke the fence, dropped a handkerchief of his, and planted a false weapon with one of his hairs stuck in it. (More confirmation: handkerchiefs and hairs are easy to obtain in intimate circumstances, not otherwise.) Inman would notice nothing on his way from his car to his rendezvous.

'When he reached her back garden, she shot him with her arrow and pushed him into the river; not difficult with a small man. Seemingly, he had drifted down there or thereabouts after a supposed struggle upstream. But he got out of the river again and found you. A terrible moment for her. She had to hide the weapon quickly, and found what must have seemed an excellent place. She was probably dismantling the launcher when she heard you call.

'Now most of this was guessed by accident, in a fit of sarcasm, by that fearful subordinate of mine, Cox. In the course of it he produced one virtually insuperable objection. What could have induced the victim to keep still long enough to have trained on him such a clumsy weapon? Was it a lucky shot? She wouldn't have depended on luck to such a degree. I can't explain it.'

'Perhaps I can,' said Peter. 'I noticed the bolt on that back gate was very stiff. You'd naturally stay in the same position while you worked it into place. And it would tend to be the *same* same position each time, so if he went there often ...'

'My boy, you've saved my reason,' said the colonel with metallic emphasis. 'A chalk-mark on the gate—the tube itself would do as a sight—at that distance, with that power, the trajectory would be almost flat. What elegance.'

They were coming through Brixton, past the Marks & Spencer's and the Woolworth's that must be about the grandest anywhere, up the long straight hill at fifty miles an hour, in sight of the huge Booth's Dry Gin sign that was lit up after dark. Peter took another Three Castles.

'Wasn't it tampering with justice to let her escape and commit suicide?'

'Certainly. We should have had a very poor chance against her in court.'

'I want to tell you I was listening at the french window when you forced her to confess.'

'Oh. Were you? I hadn't allowed for that.' Momentarily, Colonel Manton sounded almost disconcerted. 'In that case there's a great deal I needn't explain.'

'You can't have known about her and me just from the dance.'

'No. There were two more things. One of them depends on the fact that, if the light falls just so, the glass on a picture is a most efficient looking-glass. The other is that, as I remarked in a different connection, Inman resembled you physically. I found that suggestive in more than one way. Anyhow, I was right. Let me return to and complete my apologies. At our tea-party, I asked you some misleading questions and made one grossly misleading remark. I had to: it would never have done for you to find the answer before we could make our move. Your friend Mr Langdon was the first person I dismissed from consideration. The murderer was Evans, who, as you must have heard, telephoned Hodgson in a voice that struck Hodgson as disguised. Langdon is an accomplished mimic. No such person would ... but I need say no more.

'Let me just finish with Langdon, in case you hear malicious talk. Cox was very keen on him as a suspect as soon as I told him I thought I remembered some scandal involving a man called Langdon—as you and I agreed, it's a name that sticks in the mind. We looked up the newspapers of that period. He was brought before a magistrates' court on a charge of indecency with a pupil. A boy. Having heard the police evidence, the Bench found that there was no case to answer and Langdon was discharged. But,

naturally, he had to resign his post. That was enough for
me, or rather not nearly enough to revive my interest.
Cox, however, liked it. You've seen the man and will have
formed your own estimate of him and his outlook. He
persevered. At one stage he thought he'd found a suggestive
incident in the neighbourhood, but Langdon was proved
to have been elsewhere when it took place, if it did. And it
would have been impossible to establish that Inman had
known of the original case, let alone threatened Langdon
with exposure.

'This affair would make me write a short monograph on
alibis if I were the right kind of person. On one kind of
alibi, the kind involving married couples in the same
house. Collusion, or, over a very short period of time,
honest mistake is so easy. Mrs Langdon could have said her
husband was at home when he was really murdering Inman.
Trevelyan did say his wife was at home when we know she
slipped out and attacked your father. And each of that
couple said the other was at home on the night Boris
Karloff was purloined. How was that managed? A sleeping
draught for the husband? Risky. A quarrel, the wife locking
herself in the spare room? I should have asked her, but
there wasn't time.

'Any questions, Peter?'

'What happened at Christchurch, sir?'

'Ah. That was Mrs Rattenbury last year, tried with her
lover for the murder of her husband. The lover was sentenced to death; she was found not guilty and set free, but
committed suicide by stabbing herself at the side of a
stream. Some men cutting reeds nearby offered to help her,
but she asked them to leave her alone. One who was fas-
cinated by crime would have remembered the case well.
And she—she was such a one. So much so that her situation

with Inman was perhaps no more than the first she'd met
with in which murder was ... what? Plausible. Congruous.
Apposite.'

They reached Norbury, where the trams ended and the
buildings began to thin out. After a left fork at Thornton
Heath Pond, fields appeared: this was Surrey now, not
London. Nearly home. Peter's main feeling, for the
moment, was relief that somebody else knew everything
that had happened, was not shocked by the shocking part,
and would never tell anyone.

The colonel stopped the Jaguar some yards short of
Riverside Villas, produced a pigskin wallet and took from
it a folded piece of white paper with a little printing on it.

'A five-pound note. Take it. It's a reward for your
intelligence and discretion. An unofficial reward, because
much of what you did is not part of history. Spend it
unwisely.'

'Thank you very much, sir. I suppose, I don't suppose
we ... '

'No. How sound your instincts are. I now know you
know what I am, or what I used to be: a small enough part
of my life at any time, but the smallest part is too much.
That—thing in me enabled me to understand her and to
predict how she would behave, with a result I expect could
be called socially useful. But friendship between us has
become impossible, I'm afraid. It's the sort of penalty one
pays for—well, for existing, really. Still, there's always
youth. Isn't there? We'll see each other again and perhaps
talk these matters over. But not yet. Good luck, Peter.
You're a sane human being and you'll survive all this.'

The rasp remained in Colonel Manton's voice throughout. He drove his car away. Peter let himself into Montrose
—his mother was learning bridge under a powerful female

authority somewhere in the neighbourhood—and, after
tea and some rather nasty music by Frank Biffo's Brass
Quintet on the wireless, settled down to his homework. He
was just finishing the required pages of *Les Oberlé* when his
father came in.

'How elderly is that brew?'

'Getting on for an hour, Dad.'

'I think I'll make myself some fresh.'

Evidently in no hurry to do as he said, Captain Furneaux
moved to the window and made some remark about gaol-
birds always liking to see the sun, at which Peter did his
best to laugh. Gaol-birds, old lags, blokes who had done
time came up in every conversation these days; it was
called getting it out of his system. After a pause, his father
said without turning round,

'There's something I want to say to you, old boy, now
I've got the chance.'

Peter heard this with variegated alarm: had his hoard of
horn been broken into, or were the birds and the bees about
to make their tardy appearance? 'Yes, Dad?'

'I'm a conceited man, Peter. Or vain, I don't know
the right word. And it's made me dishonest. I don't mean
over money, but I wasn't straight with you about ... that
police business, and Inman and so on. He did know something I didn't want noised abroad. What it was, I was never
an airman; that's to say I never went up in an aeroplane. I
was in what they call Administration—a respectable enough
job, and somebody had to do it, but it wasn't flying. It was a
car crash that did for this arm of mine. Then one day after
the War a fellow said something about, R.F.C., eh? Game
arm; bad landing or something? I'd had a few, and I said,
just for fun, yes, engine conked as I was coming in to land.
I didn't say it was in a dog-fight, I didn't go that far. Well,

the word sort of got round, and I had to keep up the deception. I reckoned I was safe, with nearly all my mates at the bottom of the sea, poor devils. Then, when Inman met a chap who'd been in the hospital with me, and started ... Well, believe it or not, just for a minute I wanted to kill him. What have you got to say to that?'

'Not much,' said Peter calmly. 'Anybody might have felt like that for a minute. But thank you for telling me, because you've cleared up something that worried me a bit.'

'Which is?'

'Why you were so bothered about Charlotte Bryant and that doctor man.'

'You noticed that, did you? You're a sharp lad. Yes, I felt I was no better than they were.'

'Don't talk tripe, Dad.'

'It was silly, I suppose. But the other thing, the conceit and the dishonesty. I lied to the police about the height of ... well, we know who it was. I couldn't admit I'd been attacked and knocked over by somebody so much smaller and lighter than me. Too conceited.'

'It didn't make any difference in the end.'

'That's not the point. And you haven't heard the worst yet. That photograph of me in the hall, with my arm across my ... bloody chest. That was to hide the fact I wasn't wearing wings, because I wasn't entitled to them. I didn't actually have a pair sewn on for the occasion, I jibbed at that. Huh. What integrity. And the damn thing was taken just after I got out of hospital. I must have been subconsciously preparing my story about the aeroplane crash even then. Preparing it in my subconscious mind. Captain Furneaux, war hero. Mentioned in despatches for conceit and dishonesty.'

After a moment, Peter said, 'You mind about it, Dad,

but I don't. The way I look at it, you're so unconceited that you tell me some things that are very damaging to your pride, and you don't like telling them, but you're so undishonest that you tell them because they're true, not because anybody's making you, but because you want me to know, and that must be because you want me to know you. I think that makes you a good father.'

Captain Furneaux, still looking out of the window, drew in his breath slowly and deeply, like a diver getting ready to go off the top board, then let it out all at once. 'And you're the best son ... '

'Well ... I think I'll pop out for a minute, Dad.'

It was going to be a beautiful evening, he decided as he walked briskly across the Meadow. The grass had been recently cut and was springy to tread on. All that rain had not been wasted: it had been put into the greenness of the greenery, of which there seemed to be a surprising amount. Daphne Hodgson sat in her deck-chair in the front garden of her house, reading a book. He opened the gate and went up to her.

'Hallo, Daphne.'

'Oh, hallo.'

'Put your book down, there's a good girl. Are you free this evening?'

'Don't know.'

'Fine, that means you're free. I'll be over to fetch you about seven. You put on something nice and we'll go out somewhere.'

'Where?'

'I haven't decided yet. I'll think about it in the meantime.'

'Oh.'

'To hell with oh, Daph. Oh or no oh, I'm coming back at seven, and you be ready, okay?'

'What if I'm not?'

'Then I'll sit around until you are, but that would just be wasting time.'

'Big he-man,' she sneered, though without conviction.

'Big, not very, I agree; still, it's early days yet. He, certainly. As for man, I might surprise you. See you at seven or so.'

He walked back more slowly. There might well be, probably would be, difficulties later, but they would only be difficulties, like the rocky slopes of a mountain, not the sheer smooth cliffs he had thought would never change.

Nearing his own front gate, he heard the telephone ring in No. 21, outside which a For Sale board stood. Mr Trevelyan had gone away and would never be back, had gone nobody knew where, could be communicated with, if at all, only through his firm. And Mrs Trevelyan had gone away too, in one sense as far as possible, in another not so far. Peter came to a halt. Mrs Trevelyan was somebody and something that would never not be there as far as he was concerned, but not just like any other deep memory. She was going to stay in his mind without any way of his looking squarely at her. Whereas she herself was bound to become a more distant figure as time passed, in a different way those two things that were already hard to separate, what she had done with him and what she had done to Inman, would run into one and draw nearer, like a double cloud coming over the horizon into a blue sky.

The telephone stopped ringing. Peter's mother emerged into view at the far end of the Meadow. She saw him and waved. He ran towards her.